Jewel of Jericho
Rahab's Story
Fruit of Her Hands Series

Laurie Boulden

Editor: Cynthia Hickey
Book Design by Forget Me Not Romances

This book is a work of fiction. Names,
characters, Places, incidents, and dialogues are
either products of the author's imagination or
used fictitiously. Any resemblance to actual
persons, living or dead, or events is
coincidental. Scripture quotations from The
Authorized (King James) Version.

Fiction and Literature: Inspirational
Biblical fiction

ISBN: 978-1-947523-92-0

Proverbs 31:31- Give her of the fruit of her hands; and let her own works praise her in the gates.

Remarkable women make for amazing stories. The valor with which they took hold of the situations in their lives induced incredible feats. God provided for each of them. Grace in time of struggle. Mercy in place of judgement and death. Love where love was needed.

Step back in time, sit around the fire, and listen to the storyteller. May the acts of courage evident in the lives of Rahab, Ruth, and Esther reflect in all of us.

My name is Rahab. I am a woman of Canaan. I do not belong in the lineage of the greatest love story, and yet, I am here. Kings have come through me. My people would look in wonder or scorn. It matters not for they are no more. Rahabek is a strong name. I took it to myself and carried my head high. Now it has come down through the ages, the story of a whore who betrayed her people. But I do not think they were my people. The One who called from across the Jordan said I am His. He is mine. As such, His people have become my people. My haughty head I now bow low, for I am redeemed in love and joy.

Listen to my story. Decide for yourself. It is no easy thing to fall into the hands of a fearful God without a willing heart.

Introduction

Joshua 1:9 is one of my favorite verses of the Bible. God tells Joshua, "Have not I commanded thee? Be strong and of a good courage; be not afraid, neither be thou dismayed: for the Lord they God is with thee whithersoever thou goest." (KJV) Strength and courage are going to be very important for the people God chose to accomplish certain tasks. We even see strength and courage in one who is not a child of Israel. No doubt, God could have accomplished the fall of Jericho without Rahab. She didn't need to be redeemed. The fact that He chose to redeem her is a blessing that should touch every one of us. That she is the great-grandmother of King David and in the lineage of Jesus Christ goes beyond comprehending. God values each one of us.

Thanks to the records of Joshua, we know Israel crossed the Jordan on the tenth day of the first month, which would be the month of Abib. From this date, we can work forward and backward for the timing to tell the story of Rahab and her salvation. This is a love story, for Rahab and for us. The journey to write this story has been an interesting one. Enjoy the read. May you feel the love of God in its telling. Blessings.

The 26ᵗʰ Day of the Month of Adar
Within Jericho:

The Inn was full.

"Rahabek?" A thin young woman approached the owner.

"Talia," Rahab offered a gentle smile. "You may call me Rahab. All my friends do." The young girl lowered her eyes but did not attempt the shorter name. Rahab didn't push. "We have a full dining space."

Talia handed Rahab an empty crock for wine. "Is there more?"

Rahab reached for the top shelf. "A little." She jangled the pouch of coins in her side pocket. "Bless the goddess, we have enough coin to buy fresh food and wine tomorrow." Rahab filled the crock, breathing the scent of red wine. Talia reached for it, but the sound of raucous laughter carried into the kitchens. Rahab pulled the crock closer to herself. "How about I take this? There is plenty to clean up here."

Talia gave the mess of pots a silent glance. She nodded.

Rahab resisted the urge to offer the girl a pass on work. Perhaps she could lift the pots used to cook lamb stew for the guests. If not, Rahab would take care of it later. Rahab paused before entering the increasingly loud dining area. Much later, she thought with a sigh.

She weaved through a few tables, checking on her top customers first.

An unfamiliar man pulled her arm. "I will pay you for the slave."

Rahab made certain her glare revealed what she thought of his unwelcome touch. He withdrew his hand, lowering his eyes in apology. Rahab stood her ground and shook her head. "The girl has been saved for a better life."

"A better life?" He jeered. "What does that matter to a slave?"

"Talia is not a slave. She is paid for her work. She will go to Deanas for an education when she is ready for learning."

He shook his head. "Not all are intended for knowing lives."

"I will not tolerate abuse in my presence. The girl stays with me."

A familiar customer next to the stranger grabbed the man by the shoulder. "No use arguing, friend." He winked at Rahab. "This woman will not be swayed."

Rahab grinned. "Here is one who can tell you my nay is nay." She changed her voice to a seductive tone. "And my yay is yay."

"Indeed." His eyes darkened. "A finer yay I have never met."

Rahab acknowledged his compliment and continued through the room. One of a group near the middle raised an empty cup. She weaved a path to their short table. Leaning between a pair of men, she poured the strong ale into their mugs. She brushed shoulders with the man on the left. His hand smoothed the back of her silk dress, speaking words she didn't understand. His hand moved lower. She didn't need words to explain what he desired. She laughed, pulling his hand away. Several options presented themselves tonight. She'd wait to make her decision.

"Inn-tress."

Another patron hollered across the room. She moved toward the doorway and offered a bow. "Goddess bless you this eve, Ishari." She accepted his woolen wrap, placing it on a hook inside the door as the familiar guest walked to an empty table. She brought water. "You come late tonight."

"Our caravan would not fit the road to the west, we traveled north around the sea and came south to Jericho."

"You are tired. I can provide a sleeping pallet in the common room upstairs."

"Do you have any meat from the evening meal?"

She motioned toward the crowd and shook her head. "The Inn is full. I can bring you a plate with goat cheese and warm bread."

"You are a jewel, Rahab."

Rahab moved through the dining room into the first kitchen space. "Talia?" She called. She heard nothing, but when she looked at the doorway, Talia stood waiting for direction. "We have a late arrival." Rahab pulled a chunk of goat cheese from the cooling cabinet. "Do we have any meat remaining?"

"I will see." Talia's soft voice faded as she turned away.

Rahab used the knife on the counter to cut part of the green rind. The cheese beneath had a milky color. She cut fresh cheese for the meal platter. The remaining tomatoes were not as good, still she managed a few slices. A hunk of bread took up another portion of the platter.

"We have this." Talia appeared at Rahab's elbow, offering a small dish with bits of lamb.

"Good." Rahab took a piece, giving it a smell. "Very good." She added the meat to the platter. "Finish cleaning the kitchen and you may turn in for the night."

"Yes, Rahabek. Thank you."

"Rahab." She repeated.

Talia cracked a tiny smile as she turned away, though her golden-brown eyes stayed serious.

Rahab lifted the platter, balancing it with one hand. No wine remained, but she filled a fresh cup with juice from the apples. She returned to the dining area, taking a seat across from Ishari. She leaned in as he enjoyed the food. "Did you notice anything of interest in your latest journey? Why have so many travelers come out of season?"

He shook his head. "Unease spreads, but there are merely rumors to uphold it. Desert ghosts and a sense of doom. Some claim a warning to leave these lands has come."

"A warning from who?"

He shrugged. "I know no reason to fear. All cities within a hundred leagues are walled. If trouble were to come to one, others would rally. There would be little chance of victory against the great nations of Canaan."

Rahab looked across her crowded common area. No cause to fear, yet the men spoke in quiet voices, an unpleasant edge in their demeanor. "I will trust Ashteroth and gods of the land. They will protect us from ghosts and fools who rise against the great walls of Jericho."

With travelers settled for the night, Rahab crawled through the window of her inn onto the outer wall of Jericho. She leaned against the side of her house, pulled the sandal from her foot, and pressed her fingers against the fleshy part beneath her toes to assuage the ache. Her sigh melted into the chorus of cicadas enjoying the warm night.

She eased her other foot from her sandal and massaged the weariness away. The red flag hanging in her courtyard marked her home as a place of sleep for travelers. The street along the wall had four such abodes, but hers was the first when entering the eastern gate. With her feet much improved, Rahab stilled and allowed the night to embrace her. Clouds hung low, lightning in the distance. The scent of rain hovered in the air but drops had yet to fall.

A gong sounded in the distance, midnight ringing at the temple. Rahab jumped, startled awake. She would need to rise early in the morning to prepare the break of fast for her patrons.

Lightning flared once more, and a thick column appeared in the flash a great distance away. Her heart thumped in her chest, and she bowed her head. What had such a thing to do with her? She forced her thoughts to tasks for the morrow. The market would be slim, being midweek. She and Talia could travel south of Jericho to the farms. Fresh air would benefit the girl.

A rumble of thunder sent her back inside. Snores sounded from one of the rooms. In her bare feet, Rahab slipped noiselessly across the brick-colored tiles that lined the floors. Stairs on the left led to an upper set of rooms. At the end of the hall, another set of stairs curled to the first floor. After checking the oil in the hall lantern, she took the steps down. The large open area served as the commons. A small room to one side held basins for water to wash and refresh. Kitchens were toward the front, with a side door to the garden and stone oven. Her rooms were also to the front, near the entrance. The downstairs oil lamp was filled and offering soft light across the space. A beam fell on the face of a man in her bed. Unlike her thick curly hair, his was smooth and straight. She wanted to run her fingers through it, so unlike her own it was. She sighed. The stranger in her bed slept. She kept her robes and lay beside him. His arm wrapped around her and she cuddled against him, allowing the warmth of his body to lull her to sleep. He would have what he desired in the morning if he woke before she need rise.

The 27th Day of the Month of Adar
Within Jericho:

A kiss against her shoulder woke Rahab while the night wrestled with morning. It didn't take long for him to find the opening in her robes. Sleep turned to desire as he explored. Pale light flooded the room when he slipped away. Rahab stretched, satisfaction making her sleepy. A pair of squawking birds rustled within the branches of the tree outside the window. The world waking, now it was her time as well.

She pulled herself from the bed, walking naked across the cold stone floor. She dipped a cloth in the basin of water and washed herself before donning a yellow wrapped blouse with printed red birds. She twisted the sash around her back and tied a bow in front above her navel. The matching skirt rode low, leaving her midriff bare. She opened the vial of kohl and painted black swirls that curled around her cheeks and up into her hairline. Looking at herself in the glossed metal hanging on a wall, Rahab twisted from one side to the other. She pressed a hand against her flat belly. Rumal juice would protect her from a child. Gold glinted as sunlight peeked into the room. Her smile widened. The guest offered a pleasant token. She added his coins to the pouch. A leather belt rode above her hips and she secured the pouch using hoops reinforced with metal. The weight was more than she normally carried, but perhaps something special could grace the dining patrons this evening.

Rahab wasn't surprised to find Talia in the kitchen, dressed and ready for work. She was surprised that the girl had the cast iron flat heating on the coals and a basket of eggs ready to be whipped. "Ashteroth's blessings to you, Talia." Rahab greeted.

Talia gave a quick smile. "Rahabek."

"You are quick to learn." Rahab nodded at the heating pan. "Some things." The girl barely smiled, but Rahab got the feeling she used her full name on purpose. "Use a scoop of lard to prepare the pan."

Talia followed the directions. Rahab cut bread, brushed flies from a piece of meat hiding in a corner of the counter. She tossed the spoiled beef through the open door. A shadow passed the threshold. What should have been a wild dog stepped closer and closer each day to the inn. Rahab grinned. Probably because she couldn't resist tossing bits of food to keep it near.

At the sound of sizzling, Rahab turned. Talia poured a thick mixture of egg into the pan, grabbing a pot of seasoning.

"Remember to keep it stirring." Rahab directed as she pulled a bowl of jelly from the shelf. She sniffed. Sweet berries, nothing sour or spoiled, filled her nose. She added it to a platter. Talia seemed good, stirring the eggs with a tapered wood handle, so Rahab lifted the tray and moved into the dining hall. She set her burden on a thin table against the wall. She crossed to the arched fireplace, stoking the coals before grabbing the iron bowl used to heat water and tea leaves. She stepped outside, turned left. Beneath the flag that marked her house as an inn for merchants and strangers entering Jericho at the Eastern gate hung the water sack. She unhooked the end, untwisting the knot, and let water pour into the pot on the ground. She stopped the water flow before the pot overfilled, twisted the end and hooked it up so no water would leak out. The full pot took two hands to lift. She stepped carefully, not wanting water to drench her new outfit. Once inside, she lifted the pot onto the hook above the fire and pushed so the bottom was licked by flames.

Patrons stirred. Rahab and Talia served their break of fast before the patrons left the inn. The sun was nearly overhead when Rahab had time to pull the red flag down. More visitors would arrive by evening. She needed food and wine to fill them. Rahab placed the flag inside. Talia covered her mouth to hide a yawn, and Rahab pushed her out of the kitchen. "Rest. I will get what is needed from the market. You have worked this morning. Tonight, we will have more guests to serve and you will need your strength."

Talia shook her head. "I should help you."

"You have." Rahab placed a hand on her shoulder. "You are still healing from your wounds. A bit of rest will do you good. You will come to market next week."

Talia nodded and walked away. How anyone could lash a girl—Rahab seethed. Too many men like Captain Axard committed violence against too many women like Talia and her friend, Marlyn. The memory still made her stomach heave.

Captain Axard's foot kicked and Marlyn rolled as Rahab turned a corner. She drew the dagger she often carried, running to put herself between the Captain and his prey. She held the dagger firmly, even though her legs trembled.

"Out of my way." Captain Axard hissed.

Rahab shook her head. "Go home or return to your duty." Marlyn groaned behind her, but Rahab kept her focus on the Captain.

His demeaner changed, shoulders falling, chest stilling. He grinned. "You are a feisty one. What is your name?"

Rahab shook her head.

He stepped closer. "You might as well tell me. I will find out."

Rahab kept her ground, the dagger firmly between them. "Go."

"As you wish." He offered a bow. "We will meet again. I will make certain."

Rahab shook the memory away. In the two years since he'd beaten Marlyn, he'd repeatedly tried to seduce Rahab. But she had no time for men like him, nor merchants who beat on helpless slaves.

With basket in hand, Rahab set out. She lifted the woven carrier and placed it on her head. The slight indent allowed her to balance the basket and shield her eyes from the bright sun. None of the clouds from the previous night remained. The sky to the east spread clear blue as far as she could see.

Rahab followed the road, passing the gate that would lead out of Jericho, and entered the markets. A handful of stalls remained opened. She nodded at an old man sitting beside a stall of charms. A few shacks down, she heard a bleat of sheep. Carcasses of lamb hung beneath the awning. She pointed to a pair with marbled fat through their shanks. "Two-bit coin for them both."

The hag scowled. "Three finger gold coin each those are."

"You wouldn't get three fingers for the lot. One gold coin." Rahab pulled a coin from her pouch. The unfamiliar figure pressed on the surface meant nothing, its value was precious metal.

The hag snagged the coin, dipping an edge of it in a small vial of clear liquid. The liquid remained clear. The hag slipped the coin into a pocket and nodded at the two carcasses Rahab wanted.

Rahab pointed at the boy scribbling in the dirt with a stick. "I'll give you silver coin to get those to my inn."

The other woman pulled the boy to his feet with a smile. Rahab continued through the market, but nothing else caught her eye. The wine vendor hadn't opened. Perhaps she could get a few pouches from a neighbor. She turned around, took the ramp that led to the gate, and crossed through, leaving Jericho behind her. Others were on the Eastern road as well, some in her directions, some heading into the city. She picked up her pace. If she returned soon enough, she might get more visitors for the night.

Small trees dotted the rolling hills to the horizon, beyond which the river Jordan moved in its course. Rahab stepped off the dust-filled path as a wagon rumbled past. The large beast pulling its load snorted, excrement spilling behind it. She continued in the grass until she reached the first crossroad. Going south had fewer travelers. Brush had been cleared to allow patches of farmland to grow. Another half-league, and she reached the market for the farms.

An older woman waiting beneath the canopy rose as Rahab stepped close.

"Ashteroth bless you this day." Rahab used the common greeting, but the old woman grunted. Rahab moved the basket from her head to the ground. "You have much spring harvest?"

"For now. Won't matter when the evil comes." The woman's yellow teeth showed she didn't chew much of the root used to clean teeth. A colorful scarf pulled graying hair away from her face which did not reflect a pleasant demeanor. "You'll take lettuce?" She grabbed a few heads and dropped them in the basket, then turned and grabbed a few more.

Rahab held up her hand. "Doubt I'll be able to use that many."

The woman clicked her tongue, waved her hands nervously. "Take what you can carry." She dropped a handful of tomatoes into the basket.

Rahab tucked them among heads of lettuce, then looked across the fields. "Is there sickness in the crops?"

The woman gave an uneasy glance to the north where clouds hovered at the horizon. "A vengeful wind draws closer. I fear I will need to hide behind the walls of Jericho before the spring harvest is complete." She grabbed a vine of gourds and placed them with the tomatoes.

"It is many years since rains came early, Ashteroth be praised. My house is on the wall, if you have need of a place to stay."

"These will be good to press." She placed hard olives in what little space remained. "Keep them to the sun a bit longer and they will ripen."

Rahab heaved as she lifted the basket but managed to find a balance with it on her head. "You honor me," she handed the farmer's wife coins. "I will share with my parents, no need to let the food go to spoil."

"No indeed. Come again if you may." Her face paled as she faced north. "If you dare."

Rahab turned to the path leading toward the main road into Jericho. Rather than focus her attention on the unsettling north, she looked at the mountains to the west.

By the time the road turned toward the hill leading up to the outer wall of Jericho, Rahab walked among more travelers. They were quiet, foreboding travelers who didn't want to chat with a stranger. Tension gave the air a bitter taste, but she shrugged it off as the guard at the gate recognized her and she offered a sassy smile.

Passing the street to her own home, she crossed to the inner gate. Others stood before her. She leaned to the side to see, but a familiar voice made her stiffen her back.

"Allow me to relieve your burden."

The slick voice of the guard captain caused a shiver to crawl down her spine. Rahab gripped the basket balanced on her head and turned slowly. "Thank you, but no. I carry at my will."

"Stubborn to a fault. What have you against me?" The dark man tilted his head and offered a smile. He wore armor with a regal air. Wide shoulders and thick muscles. A flex of his hand and his arm rippled.

The show did not impress Rahab. Those same hands had drawn blood pummeling her friend. "I need no claim against you, Captain Axard. My life is mine to do as I will."

"I can be generous, little whore." He reached a finger toward her cheek.

Rahab backed away, lips thinning. "Ashteroth guard you this day." She offered the casual farewell and turned to continue her journey across Jericho.

"You will not remain young for long, Rahab. You would do well to save what you can for those years none will warm your bed."

His words wrapped with anger followed her up the steep path to the inner gate. The word he used taunted her thoughts. Whore. Hers was a respected profession. A home on the wall testament to her success. Lovers of her choosing. A sob gripped her throat at the thought of the captain's taunt. What was wrong with her?

Guards she knew waved her through the main gate. The intersection beyond offered six directions. The main avenue, widest of all, followed the path of the summer sun. The City Temple had been built at the heart of the city. The King's Palace was further north, a crowning jewel standing above all else in Jericho. The avenue then continued to the gate on the western-most edge of the city.

A secondary avenue followed the path of the winter sun. Royal houses of white marble glittered along the way. Two paths followed the inner wall. Banners of trade flapped in a slight breeze that crossed Jericho. The other two roads wrapped through residential sections, with many offshoots being added as the city grew and prospered.

Rahab chose the road bending northward. She breathed out her irritation from the unfortunate meeting with Captain Axard. The path curved and twisted through a neighborhood of merchants. Their homes had been built with thick bricks and most boasted gardens. Beyond them, the houses became smaller, closer together, until she reached the area where she'd grown up.

Her parents' home was part of a collection of brick houses built against one another for stability. "Mother." She called as she crossed into the courtyard. Whirlwinds with small feet thumped across the dirt before plowing into her. She cried out, laughing, hanging onto the basket lest it fall. "Aye, you are disasters determined to fell me." She smiled at Leti and Arron, both with arms tight around her waist. "Here," she lowered the basket. "Take this into the house before you knock it from my hands and spoil the treats."

They each grabbed a side and wrestled into the house. Rahab shook her head. Maybe it would make it safely to the kitchen. Leti tripped at the threshold. Or not.

A squeal sounded from above. Rahab covered her eyes from the sun's glare and looked. Her sister, Rebacca, hung from an upper window, arm waving furiously. Pleasure warmed Rahab. Time with her sister would remove any lingering dark thoughts from her mind.

Entering her parents' house felt like coming home. She'd help lay cobbles to the front door. The inside was narrower by half, compared to her inn. The first floor had two main rooms. One wall included a bench that could be dragged. Different bits of fabric had been used to mend the worn cover, resulting in a colorful mishmash. Large cushions provided seating on the cracked tile flooring. One particular crack she stepped over had formed when she'd dropped a large ceramic pitcher filled with watered mead wine. The memory caused her back side to twinge. Father had not been pleased.

Rebacca plowed down the stairs, resulting in their mother hollering from the other room. Her younger sister ignored the reprimand, as usual, and skipped to a cushion next to Rahab. Rebacca leaned over for a quick hug then flounced back, a dreamy look on her face.

Rahab pursed her lips. She knew that look—who had Rebacca fallen in love with now?

"I will be joined with Janbod. His family owns a herd over two hundred head. Can you imagine? Their house is closer to the King's dwelling, Ashteroth bless him. We shall stay with them until a new home is prepared. I don't want to leave, but it is nicer, and they have plenty of room, being so close you see."

Rebacca continued her monologue as Rahab lounged beside her. Much like herself, Rebacca had thick brown hair that could fall like a shining curtain across her shoulders. Today she had it wrapped in ribbons of crimson and gold. Her lighter eyes danced; happiness evident to all.

Rahab twined her sister's fingers with her own and kissed her hand. "What of Richelle? Do you see her much?"

Rebacca rolled her eyes. "Richelle doesn't know a good thing when it comes to her. She has been called to the palace. Three days, yet still she dawdles. What will she do when they no longer wait? Who will have her then? It is just as well my Janbod has promised himself to me alone. I would not share him with her."

"I have gone, for all you know." Richelle snapped,

joining them.

Rahab reached for her sister's hand in welcome, but Richelle ignored it.

"If you had gone, you would not be here." Rebacca reasoned.

Richelle shrugged. "Noisome business I would have to listen and attend if I were to go now. If I wait until after evening prayers, wine and food will loosen their limbs."

Rahab leaned closer. "What manner of business occupies the king?"

Richelle waved her hand. "There is talk of spies. Foreigners."

"Jericho is an important city. Travelers pass through her gates daily." Rahab had seen plenty of them, parted ways with more than she dared remember.

Richelle dropped against a cushion on the floor, leaning back and twirling her hair. "If you desire news, you should make your own visit to the king."

"I hear plenty in the inn. Those who speak. I entered the gate this morning with a sullen group."

Rebacca groaned. "What does it matter? We have better thoughts of Janbod. His mother will provide a dress when we stand before the priests."

Talk turned to pearls and fine linen. Rahab remained until late afternoon shadow crossed the front window.

The 28th Day of the Month of Adar
Within Jericho:

His hand brushed against her skin causing tendrils of pleasure to curl within her stomach. He would do well in her bed. Rahab offered a look as she dropped coins into the till basket. His eyes darkened, the pupils widening as his nostrils flared, smelling her.

She tilted her head. "You came through the western gate?"

"Aye. A long journey it has been."

"The baths remain open until dusk. The goddess Hermione herself stirs the mud. She will rejuvenate you and bless your night."

He moved a step closer. His pungent smell couldn't mask his masculinity. "And you? Will you bless my night as well?"

She dropped her eyes, allowing a touch of heat to color her cheeks. "I please my guests as I see fit."

His low growl left her in no doubt of his interest.

Rahab drug jasmine-laced air into her lungs, heart racing with his. Sweat clung to them, her pale skin a contrast to his dark. Their joining had been strong, blessed by the gods. His breath was hot against her neck, but she didn't have the strength to push him away. The heady perfume burning in sensors throughout her rooms filled her, and she drifted.

Her dreams led her into the night, following a path along the river. Moonlight bathed the world around her. She glanced at her feet with a frown. She was no longer naked. A long cream linen dress covered her. Sandals tied to her feet helped her navigate through the brush along the river's edge. She moved onto a sandy shore. Before her, the Jordan River shimmered, and tiny waves lapped close to her toes. Insects hummed as she stood twirling her thick braid around her hand.

The moon wasn't full, yet it glowed bright, throwing stars into shadow. Across the river, a great shout boomed, causing Rahab to jump. Her heart thumped against her ribs, but the other side of the Jordan remained beyond her view.

The water near her feet gurgled and pulled away. As she stood watching, a path opened. If she had any measure of courage, she could have walked forward and seen what lurked across the way. But she remained where she was, hand on her throat, letting fear stop her.

She had heard of this. The great Egyptian empire brought low by a mighty god. Laughter rolled across the expanse, rippling through the water on either side of the path and washing over her. It was the sound of joy.

"I am." A voice spoke through the laughter. Not a voice of condemnation, but of promise, and something she didn't understand. The feel of it twisted her heart, cracked her chest, drove her to her knees in both shame and wonder.

Rahab shot up in the dark, her breath caught in her throat. She untangled from the stranger and leapt from the bed. Grabbing her cover, she made her way across the room. She slid the door closed behind her. Mild light from the single lantern burning near the entrance to the inn guided her way to the stairs. No one stirred as she hurried through the hall to the back window that gave her access to Jericho's wall. The touch of cold stone felt real, but so had the coarse sand near the river. Night hung in the sky, stars, and a moon setting with the faintest hint of crescent. She wrapped the cover over her body, but through the flimsy material she still felt naked. Exposed. She crossed her arms, hiding her full breasts. The coolness of a gentle breeze dried her skin. She lifted the mass of hair to allow wind to dry the damp on her neck.

What happened? The river snaked many leagues to the east. The freed slaves of Egypt had perished in the wilderness. Their god had driven them into the sands, buried their bodies where none would be redeemed. And yet, rumors whispered of battles and defeats, the insurmountable nothing to their god.

She breathed deeply and allowed the silence to settle her mind. No nation camped before the gates of Jericho. The valley was empty save for creatures who hunted by night.

Her lover waited in the room below, but she did not desire to return to his arms. A hard bed of rock would make do for what remained of the night.

Rahab turned her face away from Jericho and waited for dawn.

The 29th Day of the Month of Adar
Within Jericho:

Muscles across the back of her neck ached as she straightened the following morning. The sun had barely risen above the horizon. Rahab groaned. Why had she slept on the cold stone? She looked to the northern expanse spreading before her. The fancies of night held little sway in the morning. She shook her head. What had she allowed to frighten her? She stretched, grabbed the window hold, and pulled herself into the inn.

The man she'd entertained studied a pair of wall hangings. The touch of light on the curve of his bare backside should have enticed her to move closer. But it didn't. Her desire was to wash the scent of him from her skin. He didn't seem to notice her pick up the basket beside the door.

Rahab walked the road from her house to the bath house pools. A bird sang its morning greeting as it clung to a high branch of a Cinnabar Tree. She tried to whistle, but little more than a squeak escaped between her lips. Levi and Arron would have to show her once more. She crossed the road and entered the first bath pool. Natural springs from within the earth fed the pools and as she stepped in, tossing her robe to dry ground, she shivered at the first touch of cool water. No one else disturbed her and as her body adjusted to the water's temperature, she contemplated a long soak. But she had guests to feed and chores to do to prepare for the next set of guests. Talia would not be able to handle it all. Focus on business would keep her thoughts from the strange dream. She washed quickly, infusing her skin with oil of lavender, and then brushed through her hair as it floated on the water. Task complete, she pulled herself from the pool. Her skin was still damp as she donned her cream-colored under-tunic.

She wrung water from her hair, twisting it tightly until she could feel the pull on her scalp. She combed the dark tresses to fall over her right shoulder, divided into three parts, and braided her hair, using a scrap of fabric to secure the end.

Rahab pulled the blue overtunic from the basket, snapping the fabric and then slipping it over her head. She tied the side cords. Glancing down toward her feet brought a clear image of her dream in the night. She lacked sandals, that was all. Air caught in her throat. Her hand shook as she nabbed the handle of the basket. What had the voice said? I am? Even more strange than her dream, she realized she wanted to hear that voice again.

She returned to the inn.

"Rahabek?" Talia greeted her at the side door to the kitchen. She raised a basket in her hands. "Your guest regretted not meeting with you this morning. He had to leave. This is for you."

"Thank you, Talia." Rahab took the basket. Two cakes of scented soap and half a dozen star-shaped fruits fit inside. She sniffed the fruit. She'd take it to her family rather than share it with strangers. She smiled at Talia. The girl could come with her as well. "You have started something for break of fast?"

Talia gestured at loaves of bread cooking in the brick oven. "Sweet bread. I was able to raise the dough last night." Talia moved to the oven to turn the bread.

The scent of cinnamon dough cooking brought their patrons to the dining hall. The loaves of bread dwindled, and the inn emptied. Talia helped Rahab clean the kitchen and sleeping rooms. Rahab brushed dust from her loose-fitting trousers. She grinned at Talia. "I'm visiting my family. Join me?"

Talia's cheeks darkened and she swished her foot across the recently swept tile. "They will not want one such as I."

Something about Talia's words made Rahab remember what she had seen in the night. Her smile faltered. "We won't know until you come."

"I will make something to bring them. Save my journey until then."

"As you wish. You are welcome to help yourself to supplies you may find here."

Rahab followed the path she'd taken the previous day. She moved the bag from her left to her right shoulder, shifting the weight of the groceries. "Mother, father?" she called as she crossed the threshold.

"Rahabek, you do not need to bring your things each week." Rahab's mother, Malicha, entered the room. Tall and slender like herself, Rahab had an idea of her own looks in twenty years' time. Rahab placed the bag on a wobbling table next to the doorway.

"These are gifts. I would not be able to use them all myself. Why should I not share?"

Her mother stood nearby as Rahab emptied the sack. She placed the fruits in a large wooden bowl. The breads and sweetcakes she left on the table. The boys would make short work of them soon enough. She lifted a cake of soap. A scent like summer nights wafted across her nose. She held her hand toward Malicha. It took a moment, but she felt Malicha's soft touch remove the soap. "It is from far to the east. From a strange people with eyes like a crescent moon turned upside down."

"You should not encourage their attention."

"I do not ask for favors. They leave them."

"If you must give yourself, why not go to the temple?"

"Mother," she brushed a kiss across Malicha's forehead. 'Always with the temple. I have a good position. I hear lots of news. You know how I like hearing the goings on."

Thumps rang overhead. Squealing voices, crashes, and then a blur of feet and bodies moved into the room. Voices burst over them.

"Rahabek," her young brother squealed as he threw himself into her arms. Leti twisted free and danced around her, reaching for a sweetbread from the table. Rahab laughed, grabbing his arm, knowing he would push free the other and obtain his goal. Malicha shook her head as he raced away, bread in his mouth, being chased by his twin and a ratted dog.

"They still have that creature following after them?" Rahab laughed. Something in her heart moved for the twins. "Where are Rebacca and Richelle?"

"Your sisters have chosen mates. You are long overdue your mate selection. Five years younger and they have achieved more than you."

"I am not in a mood to argue, Mama. I am content where I am."

"You are not. A vision rests heavily upon you, I can see."

Was this why she had come? To free herself? She could feel the cool sands sifting between her toes. No vision had ever claimed such clarity. She glanced at Malicha. The rich yellow-orange tone of her eyes that looked much like her own in the mirror, encouraged her wordlessly.

She took a breath. 'What do you think when you see a cloud hovering in the eastern sky?"

"The eastern sky? Why that direction?"

"The slaves of Egypt travel from the east."

"Slaves of—yes, my parents spoke of them when I was young. A great nation of people who disappeared in the wilderness. Swallowed up by their god."

"Rumors speak of warriors that have passed through the wilderness. Men who stand ready for battle and yet it is their god that fights for them."

"Have you seen them? Is your vision of these slave warriors?"

"I am not sure."

"You must take the spice." Malicha placed her hands on Rahab's shoulders. "Follow the visions. Our gods will give you knowledge to protect us from war. Rid us of them."

But what if I am was the greater god? Rahab remained silent.

Afternoon sun warmed her shoulders as Rahab crossed the marketplace. Red in a stall of scarves caught her eye. She gazed at the table, allowing her fingers to run across the silky ropes. Someone stepped behind her, his body barely touching her own. Unease caused her to curl her fingers.

"What lovely games we could play."

The captain's voice grated against her ears. There was no room to move forward, so she twisted to the right, masking her face as she turned to face him. "Axard."

"Rahab."

The sound of her name in his voice made her skin crawl.

"Your order, my dear."

Rahab took the crimson cord and dropped a coin in the old woman's hand. Without a farewell, she took her leave of the captain.

But he did not respect her dismissal. His footsteps matched her own, keeping him by her side. "Why do you fight me, little one? I tire of your games."

"I mean you no disrespect, sir. You are an important man and I am honored by your attention. But I neither want nor encourage it."

"My whoring Rahab…"

Her hand shot out, connecting with his cheek. Fear clenched her heart. How had she dared? His eyes blazed to life.

A man with a soft voice interrupted them. "Your accounts demand attention, mistress." The slender merchant pulled her away, placing himself between Rahab and the angry captain. She swallowed her fear as Ishari ushered her through a pair of curtains. He pulled her along a back row, through several more doorways, until Rahab pulled him to a stop with a laugh.

"I don't think he will follow us further. Not today, in the least."

"Mistress," Ishari could not hide the worry from his dark eyes. "Better to give in sooner than later. He will have you, make no mistake. The longer you hold out the greater his desire will burn. It will consume him, and not to your advantage."

"I am mistress of my own house. I choose who will sleep in my quarters. Axard will never be one of them." His name sounded like a curse on her lips.

"He will take without your permission."

"And he will pay with his life." She drew a dagger from within her skirts.

Ishari shook his head. "I fear for you, mistress."

"Thank you, friend. I know you mean well."

Rather than go through the inner gate closest to the inn, Rahab took a series of narrower streets until she reached the gates to the south. She crossed the outer band and used the staircase to climb to the wall. The width across most of the wall was six feet, stacked stone and brick marking either side. Walking the wall was quieter. The noise of street venders didn't rise that high. Soldiers moved in either direction and she would step aside when any wished to pass her. She recognized few.

The longer journey was worth not crossing paths with Captain Axard. The man made her skin crawl. She came to her inn. Deciding not to invite guests, she passed the flag that needed to hang in the front.

She fixed herself tea as evening darkened the sky. Sitting on a cushion in the main room, she could see shelves of medicines she stored. The spice mix would throw her into a heightened state of awareness. Was that what she wanted? The headache afterwards could rage through the next day. She hadn't needed drugs for the vision the previous night. The incense she used was meant to enhance the mood of the evening, but it had no intoxicating effects.

She sipped her tea. If the dream had meant something, she'd wait for another. If it had been only a dream, then it wouldn't matter.

She lay in bed shortly after nightfall. Exhaustion tugged her into a long sleep.

The First Day of the Month of Abib
Israelites:

The Israel camp spread across the plain of Moab. Salmon, son of Nahshon, a prince of the tribe of Judah, stood among the silent mourners. Moses had gone. He died in the mountains and was buried there by YHWH. For the twenty-six years of his life, Salmon looked up to Moses as his guide, his leader. Moses was the man who could talk with YHWH.

The stories they told; great deeds YHWH performed with Moses... Salmon looked to the west. The river Jordan lay in that direction and a sea to the north. Beyond the water lay their Promised Land. Had Moses seen it before death claimed him? Had YHWH shown him a vision of what it would be when they reclaimed the land of Abraham, Isaac, and Jacob?

Joseph's bones remained with them, but of Moses, they would have nothing. Salmon's heart was heavy. Moses' death cut deep, and yet the horizon drew more and more of his attention. A spark of hope lit his chest. This was why they had come.

The silent mourners completed their prayers and Salmon headed toward his section of the camp. The tabernacle and meeting tent stood in the center of camp. Each tribe had its assigned area: three to the north, three to the west, three to the east including the tribe of Judah, and three to the south. A lad ran into him.

"Are there giants still, do you think?"

Salmon ruffled the hair of his young cousin, Elimelech. "The greatest of men cannot stand against the might of YHWH."

Elimelech drew an imagined sword from his side. "I will cut them down, raze them into the earth as the mightiest warrior."

"In good time, my friend." He laughed. "You have learning yet."

The boy scowled, "What purpose have stories and lessons when battles are near?"

"A warrior must be disciplined in mind and body. Give ear to your teachers and you will be a fine soldier."

Elimelech jogged off, slashing enemies to the left and right in his way.

A firm hand gripped Salmon's shoulder. "A few tales of your learning exploits, he wouldn't be so eager to return to his own." Bezrah laughed.

Salmon elbowed his friend. "Fared better than you."

Bezrah's rich laugh drew several glances from children. "Would not take much to achieve better than I."

"What draws you toward the children's tent?"

"Ah. I come on behalf of Joshua. You are wanted at the council tent."

Salmon looked across the camp. Why summon him now? He'd offered his service to Moses but had been turned away.

Bezrah tugged his coat. "Are you coming?"

"Yes. Of course."

"My nephew is not a boy for such as this."

Salmon overheard his uncle, Meishal, as he entered the council. "I am a man of twenty-six years, sir."

"I should choose you a wife. Then such a plan would not be for you." Meishal frowned.

"What plan?" Salmon turned from his uncle to Joshua. "Without disrespect to my uncle, sir. What plan?"

"We require someone who speaks the language of the Canaanites fluently. YHWH has led me to you."

"Language of the valley?" Salmon tried to control the smile tugging at his mouth, Meishal's displeasure obvious.

"See?" The older version of himself scowled. "Lack of discipline. He looks on this as an adventure. No awareness of the danger that awaits."

Salmon held his hand, palm upward, toward Meishal. "I am aware, Uncle, but remember Joshua's words to us. Fear not, neither be afraid of them. YHWH is with us. He will never leave us nor forsake us. If this is the will of YHWH, I am protected."

Meishal covered his eyes with his hand. "Since your father fell in the desert, I have looked upon you as my own son. I cannot fault your words. Fathers fear for their sons. It is the way of it."

"Trust I am not the same wild boy you had to discipline." He turned to Joshua. "What am I to do?"

"Our time to reclaim our homeland is upon us. Warning has been issued ahead of our company. Go now to Jericho. Watch the raven's flight, it will lead you to the easiest path for traversing the river. Head to the North wall. You will be able to join with other travelers. What do they say of us? Is fear upon them?"

"How many will go?"

"Two of you should pass unnoticed. Return swiftly. I await YHWH directive on advancing our camp."

"Have you selected the second?"

"It must be one you trust, close as a brother. Your lives depend on each other."

Bezrah would be a perfect choice, Salmon was certain. "He does not speak the language as well as I."

"Is he honorable?"

"Yes."

"Then go. YHWH be with you. I await your return."

"As will I." Meishal gripped his arm in a soldier's shake. "Be safe, my brother's son."

Salmon nodded. His throat tightened, but he straightened and walked from the tent.

Bezrah bumped into him as he crossed the yard. "Well?"

"We have a mission."

"We? I get to go with you?" Bezrah rubbed his hands together.

"Yes. We go to spy in Jericho."

Bezrah's eyes lit. "To Jericho? Ah, my friend, we will be the first of our generation to cross the river." His eyes widened. "Of many generations."

"Be ready. We leave when the last star sits above the western horizon, before dawn."

"Will we have manna? Should we take extra?" He shook his head. "No. It would spoil by the noon hour. Unless YHWH intends us to have it. Tomorrow is not the Sabbath."

"YHWH will provide." Salmon laughed and pushed Bezrah toward his tent.

Within Jericho:

Rahab moved into the field of swaying plants and crouched to touch the heads dotted with purple flowers. "I will give a sow's ear for every bundle of flax you perch in the wagon correctly." Her younger brothers stood beside her. "Grab here," she looked at the twins and had to grin at their rapt attention. "Pull upward. You will feel the roots loosen. It is as though the earth tugs back but finally releases the plants to us." She gave a gentle pull and felt the ground give way. She raised her hand with the intact flax plant. "Pull for two paces and leave two paces."

"Why not pull them all?" Arron impatiently bounced from one foot to the other. "The field always starts empty."

"Because in order to plant the field in the month of Adar, we will need seeds. These plants are not yet ready to give up their seeds."

Leti, folded his arms across his chest. "So, we should wait."

She smiled, roughing his head of black hair. "No, we do not wait. Half the field provides flax for fine linen. The other part of the field provides oil and seeds for next year." Rahab pulled another pace-worth of plants, twisted a cord around them, and dropped the bundle in her cart. "Now it is your turn."

Arron squeezed his hands around a thick bundle and tried to pull. Rahab bit her lip to keep from laughing as his face turned bright red from effort.

"Smaller bundles and low to the ground." She leaned over and demonstrated for them once more. The boys followed her step by step, until they cheered, each holding a bundle of flax in their fists. "Very good." They beamed at her praise. "Now put them together and wrap the cord."

"What will you do when the cart is full?" Leti took a bundle in both hands and bounced his feet, rolling his tongue through the vowels of Ashteroth's song.

"You have learned your songs quickly." Rahab took the bundles and returned them to the cart. She nodded at the field yet to be harvested.

"Mother will not allow us to go to the temple." Arron dropped his bundle in the cart with a grunt.

"Do not break the stalks," Rahab used a gentle reprimand. "Fifteen is the age of journey. You do not have many seasons ahead of you."

"Did you make a journey of the temple?" Arron asked, then forgot his question as he returned to working the field.

It was just as well. Rahab wanted no memory to linger of her journey to the temple. She found her place on the wall, satisfied to choose the men who would lay with her in her bed. Temple virgins had no such means of selection.

With the cart full, Rahab offered a lead to Arron and to Leti. They both grumbled, straining to pull through the field onto the road.

"How can something light as air become heavy as rock?" Leti grunted as they flew forward a bit, wheels finally able to move freely on the hard street pavers.

"I think she laid rocks in the belly of it." Arron griped, then tried to pull ahead of his brother.

Rahab steadied the cart with her hand. "If you upset the cart you will have to stack the bundles again."

The boys evened out their paces. "How will we get our load up the stairs?"

"Don't worry," Rahab laughed at their uneasy looks. "I have a pull system. The flax will not go into the house. We will use the pull to raise the cart to the roof."

"A pull? How could you afford such a thing?" Arron scoffed.

She swatted his arm. "Travelers leave many interesting tidbits. They don't mind offering to help."

"But Mother says you are a harlot; men have naught for you but their--" Leti slapped him before he could finish.

"Mother need not speak with you thus. I choose whom I entertain, and whom I provide bed and victuals."

The boys silenced as they approached the gate. Iron pillars hung above, ready to be dropped at the first sign of enemies. A battalion of soldiers stood lining the street, sifting and overturning wares as they saw fit. Rahab smiled at a familiar young man. "Goddess grant you favor, Millet." She greeted him in the common tongue.

"May the coming of Ashteroth be like unto you." He bowed over her hand, then waved them through.

The twins heaved, and Rahab pushed the cart along the incline. The road would become steeper still, leading upward to the inner wall and fortified city where the King's palace sat like a crowning jewel.

"Here," she pushed a little to the side, helping them turn onto the street that ran along the outer wall.

The boys reverted to singing verses for Ashteroth, earning more than a few hollers and bits of fruit tossed their way. Finally, they came to the arched gateway into her slim courtyard. The boys dropped their reins and grunted, melting onto benches lining the fence. She laughed at them, then took her place between. A dark head with sweaty hair landed on each shoulder.

"You did very well indeed." She patted each of their cheeks. Malicha would complain about the touch of sun that warmed their skin. "I will bring your sow ears on the morrow."

"Are we ready to leave?" Leti's voice held a tinge of disappointment.

"Before you help set the flax to dry on the roof? I think not. Who else will crawl beneath to secure the sheaves to the poles?"

The boys jumped to their feet, ready for more.

Rahab glanced across the city as orange and reds from the setting sun caused the buildings to blaze like fire. She turned instead to the darkening east where mounds of rock rose to touch the sky. Standing at the edge of her roof, she surveyed the rows of flax tied to poles that had been fixed a cubit high. The boys had done well. A day in the field had produced enough plants to fill the roof. "Amazing bounty." She meant to let god's name roll from her lips, but her tongue stuck in her mouth, voice caught in her throat. She muttered a curse, strange thoughts twisting her gut. She jumped from the roof to the wall of Jericho and then slid through her window.

Eber intended to stay with her. She stoked the fire and lay the cast iron pot among the poles. He liked thick sausage rolls. When the pan had heated, she tossed the meat bartered from the field master. Tonight would be as the other nights. Whatever this was causing unrest within, wouldn't stop her.

The sky darkened before Eber arrived at the Inn. "There can be nothing outside the window as interesting as me." Rahab held her arms above her head, curling her hands around each other as the harmony of flutes floated up from the street. Sheer red fabric drifted around her as she rocked her hips from one side to the other. The jingle of bells sewn into the embroidered hem at her waist followed her movements. She turned to face the young soldier. He had made a shy conquest at first, but months of visiting had produced a gentle lover. Until tonight, when his attention lurked in the darkness outdoors.

Rahab dropped her arms and reached for her shawl. She moved to his side. A star hovered close to the horizon. She tilted her head. Why did it seem familiar? She shook herself, drawing the edges of the shawl tight, and turned toward her guest. Distracted for sure, but there was also an air of unease radiating from him. "What troubles you?"

His breath moved his chest. "Travelers came in from the wilderness. They spoke of war, of battles against the dead." He explained without looking at her.

"Battles against the dead?" Rahab shivered. "Ill omens, to speak of such here. Your travelers were sand-weary."

He shook his head. "Og is defeated. It is not the

first report we have heard."

Rahab shivered. "Not just rumors?"

"By the gods I wish they were."

"Who has strength for such a thing?" She held up her hand. "Speak not of dead armies. The dead do not move nor stand again to fight."

"What of a people we thought dead? Swallowed up by the wilderness, destroyed by their god."

He couldn't mean... "Not those children stories? The slaves of Egypt, stealing away to return to their homeland? That was lifetimes ago."

He laughed, though the sound held no humor. "You would think it could not be they."

Rahab investigated the night. The players in the street had drifted away. Crickets sang their evening song. The paths through the hills darkened to ribbons and then blended with nothingness.

"You fear they will come here?" She lowered her voice. Could they be there already, lurking in the night?

"What did the stories tell us? Their ancestors claimed this land once as their own. They kept it until famine drove them away, but always with the promise of return. Now here they are, nearly to our doorstep."

"Are they that close?"

"Scouts keep an eye for them. They remain on the far side of the Jordan. But for how long? Why do they wait?" He rubbed his eyes, shoulders dropping with weariness. "I am sorry my love; this was not the night I had planned with you."

She wrapped an arm around him, pressing her cheek against his chest. "I care about you, Eber. I will give you rest." Rahab walked to the far wall and lifted a jar from the shelves. She took a pinch of powder and rubbed it between two fingers, allowing the particles to fall into a glass of berry wine. She stirred the mixture and carried it to him. "Here, this will aid your sleep. A quiet night free from your worry."

He took the glass from her, stared into the amber liquid for a moment, and then swallowed it all. He wiped a drip from his lip against his arm. She retrieved the vessel with one hand and took his hand with her other, guiding him gently to her bed. It did not take long for the medicine to work. He lay facing the wall, a garbled snore muttering on his intake of breath.

Rahab changed into more suitable attire, doused all the torches save the one closest to her bed. She sat on the edge, not worried about disturbing Eber, but still, the desire for sleep held no sway. Perhaps a drink for herself? She could barely make out the shelves of jars across the room. No, not tonight. She left her bed, went upstairs, and moved to the window. She climbed through and stood on the wall.

The night watches were set. She could see the glow in the distance on either side of her. But it was the darkness beyond the walls of Jericho that drew her attention. Stars gleamed across the heavens. The faintest sliver of moon edged near the caves.

They couldn't move in darkness, she reasoned with herself. If they were an army, they would need light. Light she would be able to see if they were near enough. The whole of Jericho would be able to see. They would defend themselves against such an enemy.

Are they the enemy? She squeezed her eyes closed. That name, what had it been? Abraham. Yes. She opened her eyes, night prevailed. The land had been Abraham's once; could he return to claim it? How would such a thing even be possible? Dead armies? No. If they were out there, they would be flesh and blood. What manner of slaves could destroy the Egyptians? How could they destroy barbarians dwelling in the wilderness? "Who is with them?" Rahab whispered, but the night returned silence. With a sigh, she returned to her house.

Her bed did not entice. Usually, it was her monthly cycle that kept her from company, but that had ended weeks past. Her stomach churned at the thought of laying at his side. She removed herself to the guest quarter. She settled on a thin raised mat, her arm resting behind her head. Through the open window she could see stars twinkling against their inky backdrop. Silence reined in the house. The soft hush of insects out of doors lulled her to sleep.

Cold water splashed over her feet. Rahab looked down, lifting her robes from the wet. She stood beside the river, could hear its gurgling as it stayed on course. The air around her buzzed with energy. A giddy joy lightened her heart. Almost like the power of wine, but this was purer, touching her deeper than anything or anyone. Her thoughts cluttered with a million things. Dancing, singing, jumping, splashing, laughing...

"My daughter."

A pure voice opened her heart. Darkness poured from it and she dropped to her knees, unmindful of the waves. Breath stuck in her throat, caught in the gripping battle between joy and guilt.

Rahab twisted and fell against the floor, once more in her house, in a bedchamber. She gasped for breath, willing her mind to flee from the choking hold of emotions. It was wood beneath her hands, not wet sand. Walls around her were made of hand-hewn bricks, not the emptiness of the river valley. She sat up, drawing her legs close, and leaned her head against the bed. What madness was this?

The 2nd Day of the Month of Abib
Israelites:

Salmon managed a bit of sleep, but it was not

difficult to rise when the Northern Star could be seen
through the tent opening. Today, he and Bezrah would
cross the Jordan River as spies. What would they see?
What would it be like? What danger would they face?
Had his language tutors been accurate in their
knowledge of speech? Questions rolled through is
mind. He jumped from his mat.

A small traveling bag was all he would take. He
rolled the sleeping mat and blanket and tied it to the
bag. He shoved a change of clothes into the bag and a
dagger that could be used to prepare food provided by
YHWH. Or used for protection if the need arose.

Foreigners would kill both of them if any
suspicions grew regarding their origins. He put a wrap
for a turban and an overcoat into the bag and tied down
the lid. Mother had sewn two straps into the travel bag,
allowing him to carry it securely on his back. His
insides buzzed with excitement as he exited the tent.

Lights of campfires glittered across the plains of
Moab as far as Salmon could see. Though some of the
tribes had moved into the cities of their defeated foes,
most remained here, preparing for war and the

Promised Land. He hitched his satchel over his shoulder and crossed near Bezrah's family tents. His friend joined him, silence remaining between them. Salmon looked to the stars. The desert scorpion would set beyond the Jordan River. They would follow it.

Within Jericho: "Ew," Arron gasped, holding a baby away from his body as creamy goo dripped down the front of his cloak.

Rahab laughed, lifting the gurgling infant from her brother's arms. "Always prepare for such a disaster. You can't expect only giggles from the young."

Arron fled the room as Rahab swiped the edge of her skirt across the infant's chin. He grasped at her shirt to push himself far enough back to look her in the eyes. His were dark brown with a glint of sparkle. She breathed in the warm smell of him. *What if he were mine? What if I had carried him in my body?* She was the eldest of five. She earned decent money as an innkeeper. There were plenty of men to... use? Was that how it would be for her? There were always the temple dances, let the gods decide.

Rahab studied the baby in her arms. Something inside she didn't understand wanted more. No more strangers. Not the madness within the temple walls. She shook her head. "What else is there?" The baby tilted his head, a tiny crease forming between his brows. "I know." She sighed, hiking him onto her hip. He held on to her as she helped prepare the noon meal.

Late afternoon sun hovered above the horizon as Rahab stepped into the street.

"Don't you want to take him with you? Bezus likes

you." Arron stood near the gate, holding the young child. The small dog panted beside them.

Rahab grinned. Arron didn't seem too eager to release the baby into her care. "The inn will be busy, not a place for an infant."

He made an unconvincing grimace. "His parents won't return until the week's end."

"It will be good experience, give you an idea of how I felt with the two of you. Imagine double what you go through." She waved and turned the corner. She'd been twelve and enjoyed the rascals. Had helped care for them almost three years, up until her fifteenth birthday and her visit to the temple. A chill chased down her back as glow of the setting sun illuminated the temple at the end of the street. A small crowd mingled at the steps. The cry of a baby carried on the soft breeze. She hurried her pace, wanting to cover her ears with her hands, but knowing it would be of no avail. The crying ceased suddenly, and a cheer rose to greet the night. Rahab quickened her pace.

"In a rush?"

Rahab screeched as hard hands grasped her shoulders. Captain Axard's smirk stood out in the pale light of twilight.

"I have not time to get caught up in the revelry of the temple."

"Ah, ill news has led to a fresh sacrifice. May the gods be pleased with innocent blood." His gaze moved from the temple to her. "Why the concern with time?"

"I have guests to attend."

"I'm sure they are eager for your services." His hand brushed down from her shoulder, but she pushed him away before he could touch her.

"It is not a good time of the month."

His brows raised. "And when it is? Shall I make a visit to your inn?"

"My choices are my own, Captain." She stepped to the side. "I think I have been clear that you are not one of them."

A muscle in his cheek twitched as his eyes narrowed. Rahab stood the straighter. He would not intimidate her.

"You won't always have a choice, harlot."

"Do you wish the touch of my dagger? Let me pass. There are plenty of women who will accept your sort of affection." She gripped the handle of her dagger, willing her knees to remain strong. His eyes blazed. He would harm her if he could, but not today. Though his lips thinned, his hands remained clenched at his side. He moved away. Rahab sucked air into her lungs and raced into the growing dark.

Israelites: That evening, Salmon mulled as he faced the walled city in the distance. A day's journey had brought them this close. Best to wait for the cover of dawn to join with other merchants and travelers entering the wide northern gate. What would it be like to live in a city? In houses that did not move with the wind?

"Are we safe to go within the walls of Jericho?" Bezrah pulled a strip of meat from the bird cooking in the fire.

"We'll leave most of our things here. Carry light so we may blend with the other travelers. See where the day gets us."

"Not dead would be good."

Salmon slapped him. "Spending as little time as possible with you cooking will help with that."

"You lack talent yourself." Bezrah tossed a bone toward his friend.

Food flew between them as their laughter echoed through the cave. Squawking birds in the brush outside the opening reminded them of their peril. They quieted, though Salmon couldn't keep from flinging a leg bone as a finale.

Bezrah tipped his head toward Salmon's bag. "Did your mother's bag keep your things from getting soaked?"

"I think the oiling helped. All will be dried by morning."

Joshua's advice to look for the blackbirds proved wise. They'd travelled further north than he'd expected, but the river narrowed, and they'd been able to swim the deeper channels without losing their things. The sun's warmth dried them, and they found a path leading through the hills. The sun still hovered in the western sky when they settled in the cave, in view of the walls of the great city.

Bezrah placed his pack against a rock and laid back against it. "I'll settle for damp clothes and a softer rest beneath my head for the night."

"Don't forget to keep watch over the fire. I'd rather not find a beast circling us in the dark."

"I will be thankful for whatever sleep may come."

"YHWH is with us. What did Joshua say? Fear not, neither be afraid. For the Lord our God, it is he who goes with us."

"He will never leave us nor forsake us." Bezrah

finished the quote.

Lord, you have brought us this far. Salmon stared at the ceiling of the cave, noticing the play of dim shadows as light from the fire flickered. His eyes became heavy and sleep claimed him.

The Third Day of the Month of Abib
Israelites:

Dawn brought a heavy mist up to the hills. Salmon wrapped the turban around his dark curls. Excitement and fear melded in his stomach.

Bezrah pulled his arms through a coat sewn after the tradition of the Canaanites. He tried to cover his curling red hair with a cap, but the head covering refused to stay put. He tossed it with a grunt against the supplies stored in a corner of the cave. "We are blinded in this cloud."

"And they are blind to us. The sun will burn the fog soon enough. We must be on the road among travelers when it does."

"Let us pray your tutors taught you well."

"Have faith, my friend."

A bird cried as they stepped from the cave, sliding onto a path leading through the hills.

"Either we're early, or this is a day not meant for travel." Bezrah whispered.

The wider road leading up to Jericho remained empty. The mists kept their cover as they journeyed closer. As the mists shifted, the walls of Jericho rose before them. Bricks of sand and stone were stacked and mortared at least three times the height of a man. The path turned to the left and a ramp led up to the gate. Salmon pushed Bezrah toward an outcropping of rock. "We will have to wait here. When a band of travelers come, we will enter as one of them." They settled beside the rocks, Jericho to their backs, and waited.

Within Jericho: Rahab rubbed her hand against the back of her neck as she stood by the water bin in the morning light.

Talia lowered her head. "I am sorry, Rahabek."

Someone had opened the water pouch in the night and the skin was now empty. Rahab sighed. "It is not your doing." What of the flax? She ran up the steps, no worries about disturbing guests. The inn was empty. She breathed a sigh of relief as she glimpsed the rows of flax still tied to their poles. She needed this, needed to be able to weave fabric from the plants. Supplement her income so she need not take men to her bed.

Rahab froze, face toward the rising sun. When had she made such a decision? Why? "One would think your thoughts are not your own," she muttered. The sound of her voice broke the odd tension in her chest. *Water, that is what is needed.* She returned to the ground floor. Talia had spread the water skin across the ground and sat with a sewing needle. Rahab crouched beside her. "Where did you learn this?" She rubbed her finger across tightly drawn stitches.

"My mother's people taught me."

"Thank you. This will be most helpful. When you finish, take it to Sarich. Show her what you can do. She will willingly pay for this quality of stitching."

Talia peered at Rahab with an unusual gleam in her

eye. "You will sell me to her?"

Rahab placed her hand on Talia's arm. "You are not a slave to be bought and sold. Anything you earn is for you." Talia flushed, but Rahab noticed a small smile. Perhaps the young woman started to believe her. "I will go for water. You can spend the day with Sarich. There is no reason to remain while the inn is empty."

Talia nodded in agreement. Rahab went to the covered patio to retrieve the water vessel. She wrapped the large vessel with harness straps then slid her arms through and adjusted the weight against her back. She would take the shortcut along the wall, use the steps at the next garrison to wind down to the pool.

It didn't take long, as few were about. Rahab skipped down the steps and managed to glance through the slim window as several figures moved from the cover of rocks to the tail end of a small band of merchants walking to the city gates. She paused in her descent. The travelers appeared as they should. Perhaps the two had taken care of personal needs? And yet, it seemed there had been a look and a rush to join in with the others. Skulking. No soldiers ventured through the garrison, so it could have gone unnoticed. Or she could simply be mistaken. If she hurried, she'd get a closer look from the watering pool.

Morning light glinted on the wares of several wagons rolling across the uneven street. Instead of raucous noise, the merchants huddled in groups, whispers carrying on a bit of wind. Rahab pulled the rope tied to a basket that had been lowered into the well as she glanced toward the groups.

"Allow me."

A man placed his hand above hers, though he did not touch her. "There is no need…" Rahab looked up and felt her insides shiver. Though he seemed young, his skin had been tanned by the sun. He wore a sand-stained turban around his head and let dark waves of hair fall to his shoulders. He shifted his glance from her to the crowds and back to her. She gave a small shake of her head.

"It is not fitting for a man to assist drawing water." She kept her voice soft, loath to gain attention from any others. His hand slipped from the rope. Rahab pulled the bucket and poured fresh water into her vessel. "Large groups are come. Have you travelled far?"

He nodded. "My companion and I have had a long journey."

"Come. I have an inn on the wall. It would be good for you to rest and refresh from your trip." Rahab wanted to slap her forehead. Why was she offering such a thing?

He smiled, though his eyes did not show it. "Food would not go amiss, if you can provide."

"I can. Come." Rahab pulled the harness too quickly, splashing cold water down her back. She settled the vessel more comfortably as she regained her composure from the dousing.

The stranger motioned to a second fellow, one a bit shorter, stockier. Something urged her to move them from the streets.

"Through here," she gestured into the staircase leading up the wall.

The taller one lifted an eyebrow. "Is this not an entrance to the garrison?"

She nodded. "And the wall. We will be able to

move quickly with fewer eyes noticing."

"What care we for notice of these rabble rousers?" The stranger asked, then spoke to the other man. The other grunted.

Rahab urged them forward with a hand gesture. "We are leery of strangers lately. Odd things happening in the world."

"Come, Bezrah, she offers a morning meal." The man looked at his companion. Rahab noticed a slight shake, thinning lips. But they both followed as she led them to the stairs for the wall.

They walked to the side, allowing Rahab to lead them. The taller one stayed closer.

"Forgive my friend, he lacks charm, among other things." He repeated his words with a tiny smile in a foreign language.

"The only thing I lack is a way to quench my thirst."

Bezrah's hushed voice could be easily heard, though Rahab did not understand. She glanced at the one who spoke her language.

"My friend is thirsty."

Rahab smiled. "Drink you may have as well, sir." Rahab paused at the top of the stairs, allowing them time for a glimpse into the city.

Israelites: Salmon leaned against the wall, looking out the window. Bezrah stood beside him, feet slightly apart, arms folded across his chest. He nodded at the view. "There is an inner wall."

"The palace and temple make up the heart of the city. Jericho has grown so thick, they built between the walls. Have you not seen the inner city?" The strange woman asked.

Salmon had never seen a woman like her. She did not cover her head, allowing thick dark hair that glinted with red in the sunlight to fall down her back like a curtain. A beaded kerchief of some sort wrapped around her head to keep hair from her face. Her eyes were outlined with lines of black and blue that touched the edge of her brows. The sleeves of her dress tied at her shoulders and wrists, but left her arms bare, a tawny color much lighter than his own skin. She was a jewel that sparkled, and he did not know where to keep his eyes to not be drawn to her. Bezrah elbowed him sharply and he frowned at his friend.

"She asked a question?"

Question? Right, had they never seen the city?

They exchanged a glance, then Salmon offered a generic smile. "This is our first venture into Jericho."

"Have you come to trade?" She turned to the right and moved out onto the wall.

"We have traveled far, and I heard great things of the walled cities of the plains. I desired to see them myself."

"Are you part of a wandering tribe?" They had moved less than three hundred paces when she grabbed a handle built into a window. She crouched, keeping her back straight to not spill the water. She motioned for them to follow. "Take your rest here."

Salmon looked at Bezrah, who shrugged. Salmon ducked through first.

They entered the inn on a platform that had steps leading up and down. They followed her down. The room was large, two windows in the front and one to the side. The back wall stood against the wall of Jericho. Four pillars around the room supported the ceiling and offered separation between seating areas. One area had chairs with long seats. Another had colorful pillows.

She motioned for them to remain. "I'm going to put the water in the front."

"Where is she going?" Bezrah used his toe to push one of the chairs. The chair scraped the floor.

"To store the water. What do you think of this?" He tossed a pillow at Bezrah, grinning as the man jumped.

"How do you know she will not betray us?"

"I do not." The pillows were decorated, cords of string dangling from the corners. And colors, how were such colors possible?

"Is something wrong?" Her voice nabbed their attention.

Jericho: Rahab poured water into a trough beside the inner door. She dipped a pitcher to fill and returned to her guests. She found them examining one of the cushions, turning it over and pressing it between their hands. Unfamiliar language passed between them.

They jumped, but Salmon quickly drew a smile on his face. "It is not something with which we are familiar."

"Better than sitting on the hard floor. There is not enough water for a bath, but you are welcome to a pitcher. I am sure your journey has been long. I will prepare your meal."

"Your hospitality is honorable. I am Salmon. My

friend is Bezrah, though he is unfamiliar with your language."

"Welcome, travelers. I am Rahab."

"Your dwelling is richly decorated."

Her cheeks warmed. "I receive gifts from many of my patrons."

He nodded, and by the look in his eyes as he glanced down to her feet left her little doubt he understood what she meant. Were his cheeks turning red? Rahab bit her lip. "There is a room to the side you may use to refresh from your travel this morning." She led them into a guest room, placing the pitcher of water on the table. "This door leads to the lavatory. Water and towels are there. Fresh clothes in the cabinet, many sizes so you may find something that will fit."

"Thank you, but our clothes will refresh."

She nodded. "I will leave you. Return to the main room when you are ready."

Desert ghosts, she was certain of it. Sons of Israel. She hurried from them. Why had they come to Jericho?

At least Talia was not around. Rahab arranged meat on the grill as she stared across the city. More than the usual number of soldiers roamed the streets. They knew. Somehow, they knew about the strangers. *Feed them and let them go.* The soldiers would find them, and their bodies would hang from the walls. But other thoughts stirred within. She did not wish to see the two young strangers meet such an end. But what was she to do?

She carried the food from the grill outside the window into the main house. What if she were to hide them? Rahab stared at the knife in her hand as she sliced the meat into sections. Insane thoughts. She would be tormented to death if they were discovered. Better to let them go. She arranged the food on a platter, carrying it to the common room, and sat on a cushion with her feet tucked beneath her.

It wasn't long before they returned, the taller leading. The two of them stared at the food. He touched it with a finger, pushing against the meat. 'What is this?" His eyes were soft, curious. Rahab frowned. "Lamb. And curry. The cold season harvest went well this year."

The taller one spoke to the other, his hushed voice using a different tongue. They each tore a bit of meat and tried a small taste. She could see they liked it by the pleasant look of surprise on their faces.

"You are learned men. Have you traveled from Alexandria? I hear the university there is a wonder to behold."

Salmon shook his head. "Our ancestors knew that land. We are desert wanderers."

Rahab allowed them to eat while she pondered what could be done. With or without these two, the desert nation would come to Jericho. Led by a god that could speak and touch the inner parts of a person. A god who could utterly destroy or save. To go against such a god would be foolish.

Salmon stood. "Your hospitality has been refreshing. We have much business to attend."

"Don't go." What was she doing? She would be killed for certain if they were discovered. "You are of Abraham. I don't know how I know, but I am certain. Soldiers seek you. If you leave now, you will be found and killed."

"Our duty is to return to our people."

Rahab shook her head. "Not yet. Someone will know I brought you here."

"Which is why we must leave."

"Stay, I beg you. Hide until nightfall. You can go down at the wall and return to your people."

Salmon and Bezrah spoke their strange language. Bezrah's eyes burned as he glared at her. She wrapped her arms around herself. What was she doing? They needed to live, she felt troubled for their safety. But where could they possibly hide? The soldiers would search the inn. Except maybe the roof, beneath freshly cut flax. "I have an idea. Follow me."

She led them to the window, back onto the wall, then up the short flight of steps to the roof of the inn. "There is room beneath the flax. Remain here until I return after night has fallen. Please, I will not betray you."

"It will be ill for you if you do." The tall man studied her with his camel-colored eyes. Any lingering doubt cleared from his face. "Very well, Rahab of Jericho. We will remain here. Be careful. I do not imagine a pleasant ending for any of us if we are discovered."

Rahab returned to the window as they scurried beneath the flax. Cloudy skies and the breeze blowing from the north would make their stay bearable. Was she doing the right thing? Something in her heart said yes.

Several hours later, the door thudded from a hard hand. Rahab turned a moment toward the window, her thoughts on the men hiding beneath flax. She rushed downstairs as the force against the door increased. Throwing open the viewing window, she glared at the captain. "You are not welcome."

His sneer caused fear to turn her stomach. "I come on official business. The king would have words with you."

Rahab closed the viewer, pulled air into her lungs, and exhaled. Israel's God, how would he protect her now? Protect the spies? She opened the door, her face assembled into calm. Captain Axard made to grip her arm, but she offered a tight smile. "I can manage."

"Where is your slave?"

She scowled. "I own no one."

"The young woman who works for you. Where is she?" His eyes blazed.

Rahab breathed. "Not here. She is considering an apprenticing."

"Let's go."

A pair of soldiers waited for them to cross through the front gate before moving toward her house. Rahab's step faltered a moment. "What are they doing?"

"A search needs to be conducted."

"Search? For what?"

"Strangers. Accursed Jews." He spat in the dirt. "You'd have been better with me than what they will do with you when the strangers are discovered in your house."

"The only visitors I've had this day left hours ago."

"You can explain yourself to the king." His cold demeanor remained as they crossed through the gates, turned to the city center, and walked the path up the hill. Rahab swallowed the twinge of bile as they crossed the threshold of the palace. Tall ceilings and cool dark surrounded her. King Asureth loved his reds. A path created by woven mats led the way through the antechamber into the general assembly. Slaves stood in lines along the walls waving wide palm fronds. A basin on one end of the dais gleamed with red. Rahab forced her eyes to look beyond it and the thick drops on the floor. She forced herself to look upon the massive king.

Even from a distance he seemed larger than life, a thick powerful god. He filled the gold-plated chair. His head had been shaved save for a long black braid that started between his brows, crossed the crown of his head, and disappeared down his back. The robes he wore shone red, silky fabric against which his skin appeared pasty.

His azure eyes looked her up and down. She shivered, but the flicker of fear in the king gave her courage. She knelt before him, touching her forehead to the cold marble floor, and waited. A servant stepped beside her and gently held her arm, inviting her to stand.

"Do you know why your presence is required today?"

"I do not, my king." She focused on his feet.

"The markets were not so busy that your attention to a pair of Jewish dogs went unnoticed."

"Jewish dogs?" She dared to raise her eyes to meet his, then dropped them once more to the patterned floor. "Forgive me, my king. I offered substance to a pair of easterners. Their look was peculiar, and others may have been mistaken."

"Easterners, you say. When the soldiers bring them here, I will not doubt your assessment?"

"Nay, my king, you would not. But they no longer reside at the inn. Rumors of the Jewish camp caused them to tremble with fear. They departed to return to their own country."

Something crashed against the floor. Rahab jumped.

"Fool woman. You invite spies into our midst, then offer a way from our city that is beyond the watchful eyes of our army?" His voice thundered.

Rahab fell to her knees. "My king, I did not seek to hide their departure. The way down from the wall would take them past the Eastern watch. They have not had long to travel. Send after them. Return them to your courts and see if they are men of the east or spies from the camp of your enemy."

The pair of soldiers sent to search the inn entered the courts. They stepped beside her, bowing low before the king. Rahab allowed herself to stand as they stood.

"Well?" The king waved.

"There are none in her house. She does not harbor spies from the enemy camp."

The king snarled. "Captain."

"Yes, my liege."

"Take a core of soldiers. Bring me the Eastern strangers."

"I will obey." He bowed and exited the courts.

Rahab kept her head down as she listened to the sound of his feet move further and further from where she stood. Was it possible? God had spared them all? She stood still. What now?

The king finally waved. Two servants took her through a side door. They crossed a garden and left her outside the palace. Sunlight beat overhead and the brightness after being inside caused her eyes to ache. She breathed the fresh air, then frowned in the direction of the temple. Drums thumped through the street. She crossed to the main road leading down to the outer wall and her home. She ran to the strangers still hiding beneath the flax on her roof.

No other visitors darkened her doorway that day. Talia had not returned by the time Rahab lit candles in the windows as she always did. Dark descended before she dared return to the roof.

"Fair thee well, strangers?" With only starlight, she could not see more than the outline of sheaves. A moment of silence, and then something rustled.

A quiet voice spoke her language with an odd accent. "The water and food you set with us sufficed. Are you alone?"

"Yes. Soldiers searched the house earlier, but they did not think to check the roof."

Salmon stepped closer. "How did soldiers know to search here?"

"Someone saw you follow me. The king required my presence. I told them you were men of the east. That you melted with fear of the Jews and departed hence."

Salmon turned and spoke to his partner in a language she did not comprehend. She led them into the upper room of the house.

"We should return to camp."

"No." Rahab raised her hand. "The king ordered soldiers to seek the strangers. If you return to camp, you are sure to be caught."

"What would you suggest? It would not be wise for any of us to remain here."

"There are caves in the hills to the north. Wait there. When the soldiers have returned, I will let you know."

His dark eyes burned into her. "We are enemy of your people. Why do you seek to aid us?"

Why indeed? Rahab breathed. "I want to live. Your God has given you this land. Fear flows through our city, through our people. Fear of you melts the heart of soldiers across Canaan. We heard how your God dried up the waters of the Red Sea when you escaped from Egypt. The destruction of Sihon and Og. Nothing stands in your way. The men of Jericho have no strength in their spirit because of you."

"God goes before us."

"Your God is truly God of heaven and Earth. Swear to me by your God as I have dealt kindly with you, you also will deal kindly with my father's house. Save alive my father and mother, my sisters and brothers. Deliver our lives from death."

Salmon turned to the other man, conversing in their strange language. With a nod he faced Rahab. "Our life for yours, even to death. If you keep our business secret, then when the Lord gives us the land we will deal kindly and faithfully with you."

He turned and spoke with the other man, then nodded. They both closed their eyes a moment. Salmon smiled when he looked up at her. "All who remain within your house will be spared. If any cross the threshold, my vow isn't with them. If you remain true to your word and reveal no more of us, then our word will remain true." He removed the wrap from around her shoulders. "Let crimson hang from the window so we may know your place and remember our promise."

She shivered. She was doing this. She was letting them go free. Would they truly spare her family? Was there anything to do if their words proved false? She walked with them to the window and tied the edge of the shawl around the post. She pointed to the north. "Do you see the star above the ridge? It shines bluer than the others."

He stood at her shoulder. "I see."

"Follow it to the caves. There are traveling bags for each of you. Should have enough food. You will find water in the caves. I will bring more food when I come to you."

A minute later they were gone, shadows against Jericho's buttress, and then nothing to be seen. Rahab twisted her bottom lip with her teeth. What had she done? The burden of her heart was less. How could she convince her family to join her? She dared not share with any of them what transpired.

"Mistress, I have never seen such beautiful fabrics."

Talia's sudden return caused Rahab to jump. "Goodness, you startled me." She said with a laugh even though her heart thudded in her chest.

"Are you well? Was I wrong to stay this late?"

"You were well within your right to stay as long as you wanted. Is this a sample of something?" She touched the earth-colored fabric in her arms.

Talia held up a simple underdress. "She allowed me to keep what I made."

"It's perfect, and a good color for you. Will you go back tomorrow?"

"May I? Unless you need me."

"Evening meal, perhaps. Until then, I think you should go. There is much Sarich can teach you."

Talia seemed pleased with her options and left for

her room with a dreamy smile. Rahab looked into the dark. Would the strangers find a safe place to hide? A shadow pulled from the wall a short distance from the doorway. For a moment, Rahab's breath clutched in her chest. But instead of a soldier, the thin dog inched closer. Rahab went to the kitchen. She uncovered the scraps can and dug for a few morsels for the animal. When she returned to the doorway, it sat close enough for her to reach. She chewed her upper lip as she held her hand with food in the palm. A brief hesitation, and then he licked her hand clean. It scooted back to a spot near the newly filled water skin.

Israelites: "You did not tell her we came through this way?" Bezrah asked as they left the thick walls of Jericho looming behind them.

"No, but we have supplies for several days. We will need to wait at least two."

"Better than the heat beneath the plantings on the roof."

Something rustled, and they ducked from the path. An animal howled in the distance, another answering its call. They reached the hills without further incident.

Climbing in the dark proved more difficult than climbing on a foggy morning. Salmon's hand slid against a rock, pain slicing through his palm. He refused to dwell his thoughts on the chilled dirt through which they climbed. They finally settled in an alcove.

Salmon leaned his head against rock, pressing his injured hand against his coat. "Let us remain here. We will not find our shelter in the dark."

"Will our enemy see us in the morning?"

"Not unless they are at our feet. Our clothes blend

well with the hills."

Bezrah offered a sigh and settled. He dug into the satchel Rahab filled for them. Salmon accepted a chunk of bread. "Different." The bread didn't taste bad, but compared with what fell from the heavens...

"Be thankful YHWH provides well for us."

The Fourth Day of the Month of Abib
Israelites:

Night crept. Salmon knew time passed because the stars overhead moved. At the rustle of leaves in the brush nearby, his heart hammered with fear. Bezrah stiffened beside him. Neither slept. Were those human feet skimming the side of the mountain? Wouldn't they carry torches? Soldiers of Jericho would have as much difficulty seeing in the dark as he and Bezrah. He slowly fisted his injured hand, wincing at the sting.

Something scurried away as a lone howl rent the insect chorus. Those feet were smaller than human. The image of a wolf's snarl came to mind, lips drawn back from dagger-sharp teeth as spittle dripped. Salmon shivered as he rubbed the heels of his hand against his eyes. Why allow such thoughts to instill fear? YHWH had chosen them, surely, He would protect them as well.

Salmon closed his eyes again. What had Joshua told them? Fear not, neither be afraid of them, for the Lord your God is with you wherever you go. He would be with them in the dark on the side of a mountain a stone's throw from the gates of Jericho. Another howl disturbed the quiet. He was with them against the jaws of wild beasts. He repeated the words in his head. Fear not, neither be afraid of them, for the Lord your God is with you wherever you go.

Every time his heart started in fear, Salmon forced his thoughts to repeat the words of Joshua. The stars of the night drew closer, dazzling in their beauty. They began to dance, and Salmon let his body go limp.

He awoke with a start and realized the eastern horizon beyond the mountains had lightened. He could barely make out the dark outline of bushes and trees, the outline of the mountain against the brightening sky. Stars overhead were still. How fanciful, imagining their dance. Bezrah stirred beside him but they waited in silence as dawn touched the sky with streaks of gold and orange. Body needs he'd ignored since they stopped for the night took on new urgency. When enough light made the way visible, he rolled over and crouched on all fours. His hand still hurt, but most of the sting had faded. He crawled to a thicker band of brush and took care of business. Bezrah returned from a different direction at the same time.

They kept low to the ground. The city walls were far enough away they shouldn't be seen. Salmon frowned as he studied the terrain, but Bezrah pulled on his shirt. Salmon looked in the direction Bezrah pointed. Their flight in the dark led them closer than he'd thought. He returned Bezrah's grin with one of his own. He grabbed the satchel Rahab had provided them, and they crossed to an animal track leading in the direction they wanted to go. The sun was still closer to the horizon than overhead when they arrived at the cave.

Salmon dropped Rahab's satchel beside the one his mother had made for him. He traced the symbol mother had sewn.

"Finally, we can build a fire," Bezrah spoke with a hushed voice as he pulled a few sticks from the pile they had gathered.

Salmon reached and placed his hand against Bezrah's arm, stopping him. He shook his head. "Not a fire. Perhaps a torch to explore the cave deeper, but we don't want smoke to give away our position."

"You think they will search for us?"

He nodded. "If what Rahab says is true, they search further east not north, but they will return this way. We must not give them cause to search the caves."

Bezrah pulled a pouch from his bags, dipped a single stick into the dark goo, and then used flint to light the torch. Fire flickered, causing the walls to dance with shadows, before settling to a low glow. "Let us see what else is here."

They moved to the back of the cave, going around a jut of rock. It went further than Salmon expected. He heard something different than the wind moving through the space. It was dripping, sounding like water. Bezrah heard as well for he raised the torch. They both looked, but there was no sign of water. Bezrah moved the torch around, and then stepped in the direction where the torch flickered more. Salmon followed. They found a crevice in what they thought was the back of the cave.

"Through here," Bezrah moved the torch into the opening, sending the main cave into darkness once again.

"Will we fit?" Salmon eyed the narrow opening, but Bezrah was already pushing through. He ducked and followed. Though his shoulders brushed both sides of rock, he fit. He stepped into a smaller cave. A sense of awe made his mouth open as he took in the strange landscape. Pillars of rocks moved from floor to ceiling while smaller formations dangled from the roof of the cave. Water dripped from above. He heard it splashing into a little pond. Bezrah wedged the torch in a niche among the formations. A crack in the ceiling allowed the tiniest bit of sunlight to fall on the pool of water, creating an eerie glow that lit the cave more so than the large front cave.

Bezrah dropped to his knees. "Water." He scooped his hand through the water and lifted it to his lips.

"No, what if its bitter?" Salmon rushed to stop him, but it was too late.

Bezrah smiled. "The taste is sweet and cool."

Salmon needed no other reassurance. He dropped beside his most trusted comrade and drank. Thirst quenched, he took his shirt off, dipped it in the water, and rubbed dirt from his arms, face, and neck. He looked at the palm of his right hand. A jagged cut went from beneath his pointing finger to a middle crease. It no longer bled and didn't seem to have any debris that could cause it to become infected. He cleaned around it, pleased to note the pain was negligible.

Within Jericho: Morning light brought Rahab to the window above the wall. Eber crouched beside her, causing her to jump. She slapped his arm. "I offered no invite for you this day."

"I do not stand near for pleasure, dear one."

Rahab widened her eyes. "They have set a post at my window? To what aim?"

"That none may come through unawares. Not

yours only. Any whose abode is nearest the stairs."

Her heart stopped racing, and she offered him a kind smile. "Am I permitted to cook your meal?"

He nodded, his smile brightening. "Though I will need to eat it here."

With no sign of Talia, Rahab checked her supplies as she prepared sausages and lentils for Eber. She would need to travel to the farms the next day, perhaps find a way to visit Salmon and Bezrah. Carrying a tray with hot food, Rahab returned to Eber. He remained at his post but stood holding a plate and licking sausage juice from his fingers.

"What news do you hear?" Rahab asked as she used the window seat.

He took a bite of sausage. "Captain Axard remains gone. He has half a dozen men with him." Eber's brows raised as he glanced at her. "Did you harbor spies?"

"That story has made its rounds? How is it people saw strangers enter, but did not notice when they left? If they were spies, wouldn't they have gone into the city proper?"

"They are desert ghosts. They could probably stand in plain sight without being seen."

Rahab shivered. "Do not speak such things."

"There is no hope. By your hand or not, they will come, and we shall die."

Rahab could not stir compassion for him in her heart. He stood on the wall, yet he had forgotten his sword? "Are they allowing visitors through the gates?"

"For now. Although, not many are traveling the northern road. The southern gates have been busy; some are running to Jerusalem."

"I will remain here. I trust things will work out as

they should."

"Be careful. This is not a good time to live alone."

"I know. I'm trying to convince my parents to stay at the inn. All my family, in fact, so we can be together."

He nodded. "Overtaken with the first wave. You won't have to worry about the invasion for long."

Rahab accepted the empty plate. "I will bring more in a few hours. Perhaps your day will be less dreary."

Israelites: Rahab's bread kept them from getting hungry. One loaf had chopped bits of a bitter green fruit and tiny stems of something fragrant. The other loaf had a sweet taste, with grapes that had dried through the winter. Salmon finished his share. "Think it would be safe to explore?"

"Can you imagine Joseph or his brothers in this place? They could have hidden in these caves when foul weather hit the plains."

"What of the ancient ones and their ark? Could they have journeyed through this place?"

Bezrah chuckled. "I've heard that story all my life but being here makes me believe it more than ever."

"We should explore while we are here," Salmon looked around. "Who knows, perhaps our sons or sons-sons will need such a place to hide."

Within Jericho: Talia's face glowed as she returned in the afternoon.

Rahab smiled for her. "You enjoyed your time with Sarich?"

"Oh, Mistress. She has many lovely cloths. We started a gown of purple. It will be a fine Babylonian sample. She cut it from a drawing I made."

Rahab nodded. "Your time among the Babylonians has garnered profit. That is indeed good."

"May the gods be praised, Mistress." Talia's eagerness to call on gods made Rahab wince, but Talia showed no notice. "Will we have many to cook the evening meal for?"

"Strangely, no. What visitors that have come through seek the southern gate or to stay within the city proper."

Talia tugged at the skirt of her dress. "Then may I... could I... I mean, if Sarich wishes me to continue working on the gown..."

Rahab smiled. "Yes, you may return to Sarich. But do not tarry until dark. It is not safe. If you must, remain until morning."

"Yes, Rahabek."

Instead of inn patrons, soldiers gathered closer. Rahab pushed open her windows as she baked fresh bread in the oven and grilled chicken with stew, allowing it to simmer with herbs and spices. She handed a bowl and a chunk of bread to Eber as the nine o'clock chime sounded across the city. His compatriots brought her their own dishes and she gladly filled them.

"Have the soldiers returned? Surely they found the travelers by now." She questioned as she scooped stew into a wood bowl.

A man with silver hair shook his head. "They have not returned. Probably seeing what can be plundered from farms."

"I will need to make a visit to the farms myself on the morrow. The gates will be open, do you suppose?"

"The king is leery, but with no sightings of the

Israelites, what reason could he offer to keep them locked?"

Someone slammed a hand against the soldier's head. "Your king can do as he will. He talks with gods. If they say there is no reason to close the city, Jericho will remain open."

"Farmers are coming in to stay. Other country folk as well, yet they do not use the inns on the outer wall." Rahab offered a plate of bread wedges. Many hands reached.

Someone grunted. "They'd rather crowd the streets further up than stay out here. When they seal the gates, the heart of the city will not be a pleasant place to be."

The same soldier as before beat on this one as well. "Ashteroth will awaken, there will be no need to seal ourselves within Jericho. The temple priests have been ordered to clear out the pools and prepare alters to burn hotter. Great sacrifices will be offered if the need arises."

Rahab remained silent, not wanting to think about the blood of children flowing through the fingers that formed the temple alters. The pools beneath would catch the blood which would then release into the irrigation system of the city.

Dark eyes looked at her. "A pity you do not have a child to offer."

Her stomach twisted at the remark. Praise be she did not. By the move of destiny, it didn't look like she ever would. Returning to the kitchen, she spied the dog nearby. It seemed to know she stood in the window. Its ears lifted and the long tail thumped against the ground, even though it didn't get up. She pulled a bit of chicken from the stew, then clicked her tongue. The dog sat outside the window looking up at her. She tossed the chicken which disappeared in an instant. She filled another small dish with more of the stew and set it out the door.

The Fifth Day of the Month of Abib
Within Jericho:

At the breakfast hour, Rahab and Talia used up the grain to prepare pan cakes for themselves and for the soldiers. Rahab sprinkled a touch of sweet crystals on them while they were warm. "Men from beyond the divide brought it along with strange spices."

"I will wrap one and take it with me to Sarich. What do you need of me today?"

"Go learn your craft. I will refresh our supplies. Just remember, return before dark or stay the night there."

Talia paused before leaving the inn. "Do you think they will come? The dead from the desert?"

"Great and mighty things are at work I do not understand. Be safe." Rahab returned her attention to the cooking cakes. The remains of her supplies managed to fill a basket. She set aside a cake for herself, then carried the basket to the window nearest the wall. Three soldiers beamed as she sat upon the windowsill.

"Bless the gods for you," one young man swallowed his first cake in three bites.

Rahab offered another. "A long night?"

He grimaced. "Aye. The garrison cook burned

whatever was in the pot and none of us could eat it."

"I have a few more." She lifted the basket through the window and allowed them to take it. None refused, and soon the plate came back around empty. She returned to her morning duties.

Her hand shook as she put the cleaning tray outside to dry. Would they let her leave? She dressed in a sarong but hid a split skirt for walking into the hills. She nabbed supplies for Salmon and Bezrah and stepped to the window leading onto the wall.

"Where are you going?" A different soldier stood near her window as Rahab prepared to walk through it.

"I need to replenish my cooking supplies. I provided for those who were here before. I'll do the same for you."

The young man frowned. "I don't think we're supposed to allow you to leave."

"None mentioned that yesterday when I fed them." Rahab slid her bag over her shoulder and held on to one side of her large basket. "I planned to serve spiced rice with lamb."

The soldier's nose twitched. "Mother makes that. Camp cooks have no sense of flavor."

"That is why I desire to serve you myself. Here, a hand?" Rahab placed the basket on the wall and then held her hand to the soldier. With nary a hesitation, the man pulled her up. She offered a sweet smile of gratitude. "We haven't met."

"Yassib."

"Well, be near for evening meal. If my hunt in the hills is successful, there may even be mushrooms."

"I look forward to it."

Rahab danced away. All her life, a smile would get

her what she wanted. She was pretty, by Canaanite standards. What would women of Israel think of her? Did they paint their faces? Were their skins dark as Salmon's?

She moved to the hills first, changing when she was out of sight, and then realized she may have made a mistake. She could walk for miles, and never find them. Never know if she was near to the cave where they hid. Perhaps if they heard her? She started to sing. Rather than the verses of Ashteroth she knew too well, she used sliding vocalization, projecting her voice in notes without the use of lyrics. She looked for mushrooms as she climbed.

Israelites: "I hear something." Salmon tossed a leather sandal at Bezrah who lay on his side sleeping.

"The caves are full of odd noises."

"This comes from without."

Bezrah sat up, Salmon stood and grabbed a thick stick they had used to club an animal skittering across their camp in the night. This wasn't the sound of soldiers, least wise none he'd experienced. It almost sounded like... he looked at Bezrah. Singing?

Bezrah agreed, a frown forming lines across his forehead. Salmon looked at the cave opening. Who would be hiking and singing loud enough to foster attention? A woman with painted eyes came to mind. Surely not. She had told them to hide here for three days, saying nothing about visiting them. The sound drew nearer, and he risked a look. She looked familiar. And alone. Had she betrayed them? Why had Rahab come? "There are all manner of creatures hiding in these hills. It is not wise to draw attention to yourself."

The woman jumped, and her sweet smile made him wonder if it would be safer to look elsewhere.

"You are well?"

"Of course, we are used to taking our shelter where we may."

She held up the shoulder bag. "I brought more food."

Bezrah pushed past. "I'll take that." He scurried back into the cave.

Salmon kept his eye on the hillside, but no other movement drew his attention. "You came alone?"

"I did. The soldiers have not returned yet. I do not think it safe for you to make your way back to the Israel camp."

"I plan to wait until at least tomorrow."

"What if I let you know? When you see smoke rising from the north, the soldiers have returned, and you are safe to go."

Unlike the previous day when paint marred her features, this morning, Rahab's face was fresh. His age, or a touch younger, and a beautiful woman. Was this the temptation, then? They'd been warned against choosing heathen daughters to mate. By the puzzled look on her face, his silence went noticed. He cleared his throat. "What excuse did you give to leave Jericho?"

"I need supplies from the farm."

"Be sure to get plenty. They may not allow you to leave again once our camp crosses the river."

"Will it be soon?"

"YHWH guides Joshua. It will be in due course."

"Be careful."

"We have a high protector."

She pulled on a locket around her neck. "How do

you know? How can you be sure?"

"YHWH moves with us. Not as something our hands could make."

"The pillar of cloud."

"You have seen it?"

She nodded, then looked at the ground.

"What?"

"A dream. Walking by the river and he called to me. He spoke words I could here. The statues of Ashteroth have never done so."

YHWH spoke to her? Their meeting, her hiding them, had He planned it thus all along? Bringing her into the camp? Could that be His plan as well? His strong gaze must have made her uncomfortable.

She looked at the earth and dug a mark with her sandal. "I should go. I need to return in time to prepare the evening meal."

"YHWH guard your way. We will see you again."

A rosy hue tinted her cheeks, but her smile seemed genuine. "Don't forget I will set a fire when the soldiers return." She paused, then returned his farewell. "God go with you."

A moment passed between them, and she turned and fled from the hills. Salmon leaned against the rock and watched her go. This was not good. He closed his eyes. The promise to save her family had been given, and nothing within unsettled at the thought. Joshua would know for sure.

"That woman will be trouble for you." Bezrah pulled a chunk of bread and popped it into his mouth.

"My sympathy for our ancestors who fell to heathens has grown." He sat and broke a chunk from the bread. "She will light a fire when the soldiers return, letting us know we can journey back to camp."

"A smart one, that."

But Salmon wasn't listening. He watched the opening of the cave, even knowing she would not return. What did it mean, she dreamt of YHWH? A Canaanite offered a safe place to hide and honest council. What was YHWH doing?

Jericho: Rahab ran, heart fluttering from more than the effort it took to jump over rocks. She had taken men to her bed, enjoyed the pleasure they gave her, giving to them as well. This man made her feel different, an excitement for a future she couldn't understand.

A dark copse of trees turned her attention. If there were edible mushrooms to be found, it would be in such a place. She filled the shoulder bag. Soldiers would be pleased.

She returned to the path and hurried toward the farms. She had time to make up if she was not to garner undo attention.

The Sixth Day of the Month of Abib
Within Jericho:

Soldiers returned during the night, using light of the half-moon to guide them. She heard the shouts on the wall and angry bellows of Captain Axard at a refusal to open the gate. Things quieted, but Rahab could not find it in herself to return to sleep. She wandered to the front of her house and curled up on the bench. The dog jumped beside her and settled. Rahab stiffened for a moment, but the animal seemed content to lean against her leg. She pet its head. There was something soothing in the action. It didn't seem to mind. Rahab stayed until a chill in the air forced her back indoors.

Pounding on the door came shortly after the break of fast. Rahab had a firm hold of the dagger as she jerked the door open. Not the captain, she breathed a sigh of relief.

"Your presence is required at the palace."

This soldier had a hard look about him, but she still refused to allow him to grip her arm. "I am pleased to speak with my King."

Others kept their distance, though the city had grown more crowded. Nervous twitters could escalate into violence. How could she convince her family to come to the inn? She would have to visit them after finding a way to make a smoke signal.

The sight of skulls and bones carved around the doorway into the palace chilled her. If she made it through this first.

They brought her to the same room as before. Rahab controlled her fear as she faced the king a second time. A pair of soldiers, along with Captain Axard, stood to one side, a trembling man held between them. "He is not one of the men I served that morning. But of the east, like him." She took a quick look. "Their eyes were slanted."

The king's irritation could be felt throughout the large room. "Very well. I don't suppose it would purpose to send more soldiers. By this time, they have either returned to their camp or have made the road to the east." Something hit the floor, but Rahab kept her eyes down. The king bellowed at them. "Get out, all of you."

Rahab did not need to be told twice. Swift though she may be, it did not take long for Captain Axard to catch up with her.

"Not so fast, my little whore."

Rahab jerked her arm from his touch. "I am certain you have more important issues to deal with than me."

"My men tell me you went outside the walls."

"For food." She gave him a hard look. "Did they tell you I prepared meals for them? No?"

"You have betrayed us, I know it. When this battle is won, you will know how I treat those who are false."

"You will take a corpse. Return to your duty sir and allow me to return to mine."

He snarled. "Neither you nor those you protect will

remain untouched."

She trembled as she moved away, praying he would not notice. She forced her mind onto other thoughts, like how to start a fire her spies would be able to see from the hills.

This could go badly. Rahab bit her lip as she pushed most of the flax toward the other end of the drying racks. Please, don't let the inn burn. She lit the smoker, then pushed it close enough to the few stalks remaining on this side. A few puffs of air, and the plants began to smolder. Smoke rose skyward. She leaned over the edge of the roof facing the wall and screamed. "Soldier, quick." She had to turn her face away as a billow of smoke washed over her. "Fire!" She coughed.

The soldier dropped his spear and pulled his head shield off. He yelled for water, grabbed a thick blanket from a corner of the wall, and pulled himself up to the roof.

"Don't let it catch the other plants," Rahab stood to the side, watching as he beat at the few flames. The plants mostly steamed and hissed, not yet fully dried. Another soldier brought water. By the time they finished, the rack for drying the flax had been knocked down and soot smeared the roof.

"Neither of you have been hurt?" She checked their hands but saw no signs of burns.

"We're fine." Eber smiled at her.

"Your meal is ruined." She frowned.

They laughed. "We will suffer with the others tonight. You can make it up to us tomorrow."

Israelites: "Smoke rises from the north wall." Salmon pointed.

Bezrah joined him. "The soldiers have returned?"

"Her word is good." Salmon laughed as Bezrah grabbed his supplies. "Are you ready?"

He nodded with a grin. "We have battles to go."

Salmon grabbed what remained and the two of them took a path that would lead them over the hills and to the river. They crossed near where they had come a few days before. Salmon held his bag over his head, but the water rose no further than his waist. Though Bezrah was up to his chest, the current did not seem to unbalance him either.

"There are less-effective ways to get clean, I suppose." Salmon rubbed his arms. Though the sun was high, the air had a bit of cool, especially when wet.

"Three days pent up, I am ready for a run." Bezrah jogged backward as he hooked his supplies to his back. "Think you can keep up?"

Salmon lifted his pack. "I'll watch my pace, so you don't fall behind."

Laughter followed them as they started to run. Within a few hours, the tents of camp spread across the land as far as they could see. Home.

Joshua met them. Salmon recognized the tall figure standing at the edge of the camp. Eldest of the Israelites save for Caleb, Joshua stood straight, un-withered by time. His beard remained dark, though peppered with gray. The silver mantle of leadership marked his position. Salmon shook his head, smiling. How had Joshua known they would be arriving at this time?

"YHWHs blessings to you this day." Joshua greeted.

"It is good to return." Salmon accepted a skin of water, taking a full drink and handing it to Bezrah.

Of the elders who exited Egypt, Joshua and Caleb alone remained. Salmon's father, Nahshon, captain of the soldiers of Judah, had died in the desert when Salmon was a boy. Meishal, Nahshon's younger brother, had taken in mother and the children. Looking at Joshua now, he would be hard pressed to say Meishal was younger by decades.

Joshua grasped their shoulders. "Take a short rest. Have supper with me in my tent. I will hear your news."

As they drew closer to camp, Salmon noticed the activity, signs the camp intended to move shortly.

Joshua nodded before he could ask a question. "We move to the Jordan in the morning."

Bezrah laughed. "We could have waited for you there."

Salmon shook his head.

Bezrah ate from the bird and wiped his chin on his sleeve. "We could see the entire city. Two walls, inner and outer. Palace and temple lie near the center, upon a hill."

Joshua leaned toward them. "And the people?"

"Fear. They know of the defeat of Og, along with the cities we possess across the plains. Truly, YHWH has given all the land into our hands."

"They did not take notice of you?"

Bezrah raised his brows and looked at Salmon.

"An innkeeper on the outer wall took us. She offered food and water. When she took note of soldiers searching in the streets, she hid us on her roof."

Bezrah grunted. "Beneath flax. Do you know how buggy those plants get as they dry?"

"She saved our lives."

Bezrah waved, "Tell him what you promised."

Salmon took a breath as he looked at Joshua. Why was he anxious? "She asked a boon of us. Since she provided sanctuary and protection of our lives, she asked that her parents and brothers and sisters be saved in return."

"She turned on her own people?"

Bezrah watched them both. "He agreed to it."

Salmon straightened. "It was the right thing to do at the time."

"And now?" Joshua asked.

Salmon nodded. "It is still the right thing to do. If she is faithful, then so we should be."

Joshua pulled on a braid in his beard. "YHWH moves in mysterious ways. If you have made a promise, you will keep it. How will you know which place is hers?"

"The inn is built on the wall. A crimson cord hangs from the upper window. We will bring them out from there when the battle begins."

"I pray she remains faithful. Will be interesting to meet her." Joshua stood. "We will make a temporary camp at the Jordan River in preparation to cross."

"We will not cross tomorrow?"

"No. Great deeds await us. We shall prepare ourselves, sanctify ourselves as the children of YHWH. Great and mighty deeds have brought us to this place."

Salmon walked to his family tents beneath the stars. The quarter moon shone bright as it plunged to the west. The pillar of fire hovered in the distance, above the Tabernacle. Had YHWH drawn a heathen to Himself? What did it mean, that He would do such a thing?

The carts were loaded. It would be a simple thing to add the tent and bedding in the morning. Tonight, he would sleep in familiar space. He laid down with a sigh. The comfort of his own bed.

The Seventh Day of the Month of Abib

Children ran past over the rocks, nimble as goats on the mountains. Salmon laughed, wrapping an arm around his mother, Bilhah, to keep her steady on her feet. "They are eager to swim in the waters of the Jordan."

She patted his cheek, "As you would have been at their age."

"Without a doubt. For now, I can wait until we have to cross again."

"What was it like, this city of Canaan?"

He shrugged. "Travelers come a fair distance to pass through, heading to lands west. A great sea lies beyond the hills."

"I wonder if the same sea fed the Nile?"

"You will have to tell me if the people look like the Egyptians."

She grinned. "I do not remember much; I was sixteen when we departed."

"The woman I met wore colorful streaks around her eyes, to her temples."

"Odd markings for her face."

"They are an odd people." He glanced in the direction of the tabernacle, though it was out of his sight. "Their temple stood high in the city."

"We will see much as we move through these places. YHWH protect us, I would not wish to see any of our people bow to foreign gods. It is why we must remain free of them."

Something in her tone darkened his mood. "What do you mean?"

"I heard of the woman you met, promising her salvation." She tisked. "Why would you offer a way to bring their gods into our midst?"

"Fear of YHWH led her to help us. Would you rather we'd been captured by enemy soldiers?"

"I'd rather you had not gone."

"Joshua has heard our tale. He says YHWH has a plan with this woman. If she renounces her gods and submits to the way of YHWH, why should she not be brought in with us?"

"Indeed, it goes beyond my understanding. I simply pray you will be careful. This woman has your attention, which may be her purpose."

He kissed her temple. "I will be fine, mother. I promise you have naught to fear."

Jericho: Rahab hung the last of the linens on the line between her windows. Bells pealed across the city, causing her to drop one of the wooden hooks. She scampered to a front window. Torches along the avenue to the inner gate had been lit. They were calling inhabitants of Jericho to a temple gathering. She dropped her head against the cold stone of the wall. She knew too well where this night would lead. And she had no desire to partake in it.

She dressed anyway, wrapping herself in one of her silken gowns from the east. The wrap crossed beneath her breasts, and she tied a tight bow. The sleeves billowed around her fingertips, and she slid gold bangles onto her arms. The crimson color of the gown was sure to get her noticed, which she wanted. The King's men would see her attending. "No need to give cause for them to doubt my loyalties." She frowned at her image in the reflecting glass. Why were lies causing her insides to quiver? She applied blue and red kohl to her eyes and used stain on her lips. She stepped back and stared at the image before her. The red band above her eyes and blue beneath lit the caramel color of her eyes. Her skin seemed paler than usual against the red of her lips. She twisted her hair into coils and pinned it up.

She was but one of a thousand others, garish in their presentation at the temple. Rahab slipped past an embracing couple. Fear of what lay beyond the walls heightened the emotion driving the night. Large bowls of flame flickered on columns. Musicians danced among the revelers. Musical strains from the lyre, pandouris, and diavolos rose above the cries of the people. Rahab twirled, the clang of bangles on her arms adding to others. A part of her wanted to join further, but the sight of passions erupting on the steps of the temple turned her stomach.

"You were made for such a night as this."

Hands she did not want to feel wrapped around her middle, seeking to familiarize themselves with her chest. She wrenched herself from the arms of Captain Axard. "No permission has been given you." She hissed, but it did not stop him from drawing her toward him, hands firm on her arms.

His eyes burned, and the bitter in her stomach rose

into her throat. "Fight me, my little whore. It will be all the better." He was stronger, pulling her close enough to bite the skin beneath her ear.

Rahab cried out in pain. Something tore them apart. Rahab felt herself twirled, caught up in a number of arms, passed to another, dancing far from the captain.

"Go now." A friendly voice whispered in her ear as something was draped over her. "This may protect you from his sight, for a time. He searches for you with great vengeance." She was pushed from the crowd.

Rahab drew the cloak over herself and stumbled into the empty streets. What had happened? She pressed cloth against her stinging neck. She ran, not using the main avenue where Captain Axard could easily overtake her. She paused, pulling the dangles that clanged from her arms, dropping them in the dirt. Clouds passed over the quarter moon as she reached the inner gate. She crouched beside a building. Captain Axard paced the walkway before the ramp leading up to the gate. She pulled the cloak around her as best she could, praying none of the bright crimson would garner attention.

Torchlight shimmering on his armor and the cape indicating his elite status billowed behind him as he moved. His was the image of a strong, successful male, and it didn't take long to capture the attention of others. A pair of females joined him. Though she could not hear, he seemed opposed to their attention. At first. They dared to move closer and closer, teasing him, until he grabbed them up in his arms and stalked away to the shadows.

Rahab ran.

JEWEL OF JERICHO

The Tenth Day of Abib
Israelites:

Trumpets sounded through the camp as dawn kissed the eastern sky. Salmon stood beside his mat and donned the white robes woven by Bilhah. Three days of fasting and cleansing had brought them to this point. Dirt had been washed away and he carefully folded his sleeping blankets without disturbing the dust. A second round of trumpets called as he tied his possessions to the family cart. He moved with the other men toward the staff of a Levite.

Excitement energized the air. Battles had been fought, yes; but this was different. Anyone who dared speak kept his voice to a whisper, only the sound of locusts rousing themselves at first light could be heard. Until the staff struck a stone three times. With the weight of Meishal's hand on his shoulder and his younger brother, Sepher, at his side, Salmon listened for direction.

"The Ark of the Covenant of YHWH will be carried by priests to the Jordan River. As soon as it is seen, the procession of tribes will begin." The man's voice sounded loud enough for all to hear him. "You will set out from your place and follow. The first wave shall remain two thousand cubits from the Ark. Do not go near it. You do not know the way, therefore the Ark of YHWH will guide."

Salmon felt Meishal's hands shake. "Raise the standard of the tribe of Judah." Servants scuttled, and then the blue flag waved in the breeze rising from the river. In the distance, he heard trumpets blowing, the eastern camp had set to foot in the wake of the Ark.

"Come." Meishal grinned with delight. "Let us cross into the land of our ancestors."

Salmon glanced at Sepher. The younger man wore a bright smile. "Our home."

There was no dampening the excitement.

Salmon pulled on the yoke of the oxen, clicking his tongue to direct the beasts working in tandem. Bilhah and his sister, Elia, walked with the women and children. Though Bilhah was in her fifties, she could easily keep up with the others.

Bezrah ran to him, tugging his cloak. "You must see this." His eyes gleamed with excitement.

Salmon pulled another man to lead the cart and ran with his friend. Sepher followed them

Bezrah babbled with excitement. "We've heard of the river crossing, but we've never seen it. Moses, of course we expected miracles of him, but now Joshua? I've known Joshua my entire life."

"What hap--" They crested a rise and words slipped from Salmon's mind. The great Jordan River lay before them. Priests with the Ark stood where water should be. But it wasn't. In fact, the tribe of Reuben moved through a channel that had opened from the western to the eastern banks of the river. They walked on what appeared to be a path of grass. The waters of the river beat against an invisible hand. A boat, passengers kneeling on the sides, witnessed the crossing.

Sepher, a few inches taller, wrapped his arm across Salmon's shoulders. "YHWH be praised. They were scared before; this will terrify their bones."

Bezrah breathed deeply. "Ah, that my eyes would never forget what they have seen this day."

Salmon stood still a moment, allowing awe to hold him. But the excitement of those already walking between the walls of water drew him. "We will marvel yet when we walk upon the riverbed. Hurry, they are near to announcing the second wave." They grasped wrists in a common farewell. "I will see you in the Promise Land."

Bezrah shook with joy. "May its milk and honey flow evermore."

Within Jericho: Rahab kept to the inn three days, jumping at every noise. A scab had grown over the wound on her neck. The soldiers sensed her fear, standing watch at her window. She provided for them as she could, offering spices to add flavor to the garrison stew and bread for sopping. Dog wandered indoors. It kept her company.

But Axard was occupied. The Israelites had taken camp on the other side of the Jordan, waiting patiently. It was a good plan, Rahab reasoned when she wasn't allowing fear to hinder her. Revelries of the other night could not hide the terror that gripped Jericho. Deaths and unwarranted violence kept the soldiers busy.

"Rahab, where are you hiding the girl?" A woman's voice called from the main living area.

Rahab carried an empty breadbasket into the room.

"Sarich? What brings you outside the main wall?"

"Your girl, I've not seen her in two days. There is no cause to keep her from learning."

Rahab tightened her grip on the basket. "Talia? Has she not been staying with you?"

"Not since the morning after the temple. You sent soldiers to bring her back to you."

Rahab shook her head. "I sent no one."

"Then where is she?"

Her heart dropped as anger surfaced. "Were they Captain Axard's men?" What would they do to her in three days? She closed her eyes. "How could I not have known?"

"What has happened to her?"

Rahab placed the basket in a corner. "I will find her and bring her back. She will be safe here."

Sarich shrugged. "I hope she is safe."

Rahab refused to believe otherwise. She went to the wall. Though she was not familiar with the small group of soldiers, she put on a knowing smile and tilted her head. "I wish to find Captain Axard."

"He is not a man to trifle with," a red-haired soldier warned.

"Is he at the garrison?"

Another man shook his head. "Saw him heading to the Lone Lady this morning."

"I pray he will still be there." She stretched her hand and waited for someone to help her through the window. Once they obliged, she hurried toward the northern stairwell.

Finding him did not take much effort. She stood in shadows, watching his dour features as he drank a flagon of ale. She breathed for courage. He didn't notice her until she stood beside the table. His eyes locked on her as he slowly placed his flagon down. Rahab breathed. "Where is Talia?" She clutched her fists. His dark, cold eyes sent a shiver coursing down her back. Pressing her nails into the palm of her hands helped keep emotion playing across her face.

Captain Axard sat straighter. "She is a stranger in Jericho."

"She is under my protection."

He dabbed at the corner of his mouth with the tablecloth before standing. "If you were under my protection, your words would mean something."

"Return her."

"Or what?" He dropped a coin on the table and raised his hand to the proprietress across the room.

"I will find someone to help. You can't take people."

"Unless you can return life to the dead there is no point in finding anyone. You would do better appealing to the goddess at the temple, but you best do it before the slew covers her up."

Rahab spat on the table and Captain Axard grabbed her arm. "Insult will not go unpunished."

"Your men had no right to take Talia."

The proprietress joined them. "Is all well, my Lord?"

Captain Axard released Rahab. "It will be, once I have what I want."

Rahab turned and walked away. Talia dumped at the slew? What if she were still alive? She'd be burned with the waste of Jericho. Rahab hurried for the path leading toward the dumping ground.

A scarf wrapped around her nose and mouth did

little to block the rancid odor. Rahab closed her eyes. Talia's body sprawled among waste. There was no means to retrieve her, nor reason to. She was dead. A sob caught in her throat. Talia's wasn't the only one. Bile burned her stomach. She staggered back, turned, and vomited.

Fear of violence transpiring within the walls of Jericho pulled her back into the city.

Dassub and Malicha needed to listen to reason, for no other purpose than to remove themselves from the violence. What if someone decided they wanted the house? Rahab hurriedly returned to the inn first. She washed the rancid scent from her body using dry salts, then she donned dark clothes. Though the warm weather did not need a heavier cloak, she wrapped herself in a gray garment, covering her head with the hood.

Chaos rammed through the streets of the city. Rahab pressed against the side of a house as two large men fought in the dirt, crashing through the front of a wine room. Above the sound of brawls rose cries, screams of madness tinged with fear. She grabbed someone running past. "What has happened?"

"They have come. The waters parted to let them in." The woman covered her mouth. tears had drawn black streaks down her face.

Rahab frowned. "What water?" But the woman ran past.

Ishari fell next to her. "Merchants entering the city brought word this morning. The Jordan has ripped in half. It is as the Egyptians." He coughed, gasping.

Rahab watched in horror as spittle dripped from one side of his mouth. She crouched beside him, grabbing his shoulders. "What have you done?"

"Better this than to drown in the wave to come."

Bells toiled above the chaos; an angry sound meant to override the madness gripping Jericho. Ishari dropped his head to the dirt, eyes open though death had taken him. The clatter around her changed.

Rahab looked up to see an emissary from the king rolling down the avenue of the palace. Trumpets blew and bells pealed. She looked around. It seemed to work. Rage was calming. Tears dripped from her eyes as she stepped from Ishari's body. She ran for her parent's house.

"Why should we fear beasts from the desert?" The king's crier stood upon an elaborate chaise led by four beasts. "Ashteroth has promised to aid us. Molech has come. Gather your sacrifices, give unto Molech that he may repay you tenfold. When the sun strikes the noon hour, prepare for the Parade of Souls."

Rahab reached the house as the royal proclamation traveled through their section of town. The mission succeeded; calm restored for a time. The hope of the gods' intervention permitted what was to come. Rahab shook her head. No help would come of gods made with wood and brick. The God of Israel had no such limitation.

Malicha ushered her inside and barred the door. The twins stared at her with round eyes.

"This is madness." Rahab pulled her to the kitchen area, away from little ears.

"Death has come."

Rahab shook Malicha. "Come to the inn. It is quieter between the walls."

"Dassub will not permit us to leave the house. He

has gone for food." She gave a nervous glance at the back window. "We have a cellar to store food for a bit."

"You will be safer away from this place."

Pounding at the door caused the boys to screech. "Send them upstairs." Malicha pushed past Rahab.

Leti jumped to his feet, the baby Bezus wailing in his arms. Malicha took the infant and pushed the twins toward Rahab.

"What are you doing?" Rahab yelled as she pushed the boys onto the stairs. She gave them a hard look. "Go." She returned attention to Malicha. "What are you doing?"

Malicha pulled the locks that barred the door. "They have come for the Parade of Souls."

Rahab ran to her mother's side. "His parents aren't even here to give permission for such as this." She tried to grab the child back.

Malicha pushed her away. "You would stop what god demands? Service to the temple is an honor."

Rahab reached again, and Malicha struck Rahab's cheek with the back of her hand. "You have never understood service to the temple. Go to Arron and Leti. They need someone."

Rahab cried, running for the stairs. She heard the creak of the door opening, and the cries of Bezus moved beyond the house. She pulled Arron and Leti close, wrapping her arms protectively as they sobbed against her.

When the sun reached overhead, bells rang across Jericho once more, shouts filled the air. Rahab stood in the shadow of the door of her parent's house as a parade of priests and soldiers marched through the street. Babies shrieked, pulled from their mother's arms. Toddlers kicked and screamed against the heavy arms of soldiers to no avail. The parade marched on. Virgins of the temple danced along the outskirts of the procession.

Rahab turned away as the sour in her stomach threatened to spew from her mouth. "I am going home." She spoke to Malicha, but would home be far enough away to not hear what was happening in the temple? To not smell?

"Be careful."

She sneered. "The captain is busy with this foolishness."

"It is not foolishness. A great evil lies at our doorsteps. The gods are all that can save us. Surely the children will be able to waken them."

Tears in her mother's eyes weakened the power of her words. Bezus was somewhere among the crowd milling its way through Jericho. The warm little body that had curled against her was on his way to be sacrificed in the temple. Rahab couldn't allow her thoughts to dwell on him. She kissed her mother's cheek. "When things get hard here, come to the inn. Bring everyone with you. Force Richelle and Rebacca if need be."

"There is no purpose in our coming to the inn. I don't understand why you keep asking."

"Keep it in mind anyway." Rahab used the darker, narrower streets to make her way to the inner gate. Every footstep she heard caused her heart to trip. She wrapped her hand around the hilt of her dagger. She would use it to protect herself against the captain.

But their paths did not cross. She waited at the inner gate as a large caldron made its way through the gate and down again.

"What are they moving?" She asked Eber, who stood guard with a solemn face.

His body remained rigid. "They will melt wax to seal the outer gates."

"Seal the gates? What of travelers? That road is a popular throughway."

"Matters not. The gods preserve us. We will stand firm in this place."

"Have they warned any of the farmers that remained in their fields? Will they have time to get to safety?"

"You've seen how thick the streets are with people. They should send any who are not of Jericho out. We will have to provide for them until this blight has been laid low."

"You sound more hopeful than last we talked."

"We will destroy ourselves from the inside out if we do not hold our tongues. Twenty-eight bodies since this morning."

Rahab closed her eyes. Even more at the slew. The line began to move. "May the wisdom of our king be well for you." Rahab said goodbye to Eber.

Rahab hurried on as the inner gateway opened. Would she be able to see the Israelites from her windows on the wall? The wall was busier than usual, but the fields to the north and west remained as they always were. Winds blew, white clouds moved against blue sky, and starlings chirped as they sorted through the grains laying in waste at the base of wall. A lovely day, doom tainting its edges. Even in the warm sun, Rahab shivered. She thought of Talia and Bezes and wept.

Israelites: Less than a week ago, he and Bezrah had crossed further north using a shallow section of the river, but Salmon could not imagine crossing the river on dry ground. Seagrass bent beneath their feet. Travelers on the water turned their ships and drove the oar-bearers with fear. The path was plenty wide for animals pulling their burdens, sheep and cattle, horses, and people young and old. A boy was able to stick his hand into the wall of water before being pulled back in line by a parent. The water was a greenish gray color. Silver fish darted close to the hand of YHWH, while other shadowy things lurked beyond their view.

The valley of Jericho spread before them as they walked the incline of the western shore. Salmon sought for Bilhah and Elia in the lines, putting his arm around his mother to assist her up the incline. Meishal leaned close to Rashid, his eldest son, and Elimelech, then pointed to where Joshua stood upon an outcropping of rock.

"What's going on?"

"Each tribe has selected a member to pull a rock from the riverbed. Come, let us set camp in this place. We will be here many days."

By evening, campfires twinkled like stars across the valley. Stakes had been driven deep, securing their tents to their land. Salmon sank onto a rock beside Rashid, across from Meishal and Bilhah.

Sepher played a hollowed reed pipe, but Meishal stilled his hand when the tune turned playful. "Not tonight. Not yet. We have a difficult task before us."

"How will Canaan be difficult when it is YHWH

that brings us here?" Sepher held the pipes in his lap.

"I do not speak of battle. Joshua has met with the elders. Tomorrow we are to go to the healer tents."

"Why?" Rashid leaned forward.

"Healers have been charged with making flint knives, thin and sharp for circumcision."

Salmon frowned. "What exactly does that mean?" Details did not comfort.

"But why?" Sepher protested for them all.

"God covenanted with Abraham, and the practice of circumcision was a sign of obedience to that covenant. When we came out of Egypt, God commanded all males to be circumcised, but the practice was not followed in the wilderness. We have returned to inherit what was promised to our ancestors. The circumcision is an act of obedience, a brief pain for all the blessing that is to come."

Sepher gulped. "What if he misses?"

Meishal chuckled. "The healer will not miss. The hand of God is with him."

Within Jericho: Night brought certainty that the Israelites had moved into the valley. Rahab sat in her window, watching as campfires flickered to life across the valley. She wrapped her hand around the crimson scarf that dangled like a cord in the open window. Would they remember? The distance glowed brighter than moonlight. What would tomorrow bring?

Rahab turned to look across her open room. It hadn't been much when she purchased it from a merchant leaving for Jerusalem. She draped curtains across walls with broken plaster. Rugs and carpets covered worn patches of flooring. Doilies and brick-abrack became signs of prestige. That giving herself to the travelers hadn't been a waste. What would come of it all? If Salmon and Bezrah followed through, they weren't likely to want to carry her divan. A few bags perhaps. "Something to do on the morrow." Her voice sounded odd in the quiet of the moonlit night.

She returned her attention to the valley. What were they doing? Could any of them see her in the shadows of the wall? Could they see the soldiers of Jericho trembling outside her window? Rahab continued to watch until her eyes grew dreary with sleep. She slipped through her still house, down the stairs, to her bedroom. Perhaps she would dream of Him, the one whose voice reached for her across the Jordan.

The Eleventh Day of the Month of Abib
Within Jericho:

A low bell rung through the foggy morning. Rahab crawled through the window onto the wall. Garrison numbers had increased through the night, their voices disturbing her peace. She slunk close enough to hear without being seen.

"—in the night, as if dogs can see in the dark."

"Would have been better to run to Jerusalem. Has wider walls."

A third man grunted. "The king has locked us away. None may come or go. Those who beat upon the gate are to be shot down."

"What good are arrows against ghosts and demons?"

"Let them come. They will rush against the flow of their own blood."

Rahab heard someone pound the metal helmet of the soldier.

"What do you mean by your taunt? The enemy lies in ear shot. Without the gods' intervention, if they do not travel north of here, what hope do we have?"

Jericho would not be passed. Rahab wrapped her dark shawl around her head. She crept back to her house.

By midmorning, the clouds cleared. Blue sky shone above. Spring flowers bloomed in the garden. Beauty surrounded them, and yet an ill temper beleaguered the city. Soldiers at the inner gate offered no salutation as they waved her through. Wailing from the temple rang louder than its bells. How many children had they slaughtered? What did they expect from more bloodshed? Should not the gods have moved by now? Or did they tremble in fear as the inhabitants of Jericho, before the great God of Israel? Rahab hurried to her parents. She was expected in the blood tents before evening calls rang out.

"Rahab," Leti raced through the archway, skidding to a halt beside her. "Did you see them? There are so many they lay in the streets like beggars."

Arron pushed Leti to the side. "What of the enemy? Do they wait at the wall? How many can you see? Mother will not allow us to visit you."

She ruffled both heads. "Is she within? I desire to speak with her."

"The answer will not change." Malicha leaned against the door jam, arms folded across her chest.

"You would be safer at the inn." Rahab walked to her mother.

"From what?"

Rahab waved at the street. "From those who have little, even less to lose." She lowered her voice. "The streets outside the inner gate are not given over to squatters. Less risk for all of us."

"We have not been troubled."

Rahab sighed. How could mother be so stubborn? "My monthly cycle has come. Find me at the blood tents if you wish to change your mind."

"By Ashteroth's grace this will be over before you leave the tents."

"The god has done nothing yet, though innocent blood flows in his pools."

Her mother's hand struck Rahab's cheek with a resounding crack. Rahab gasped, pain tingling across her face. "What has come over you? You speak against our gods when we need them to answer our cry."

Rahab lowered her head. "What if they are deaf?"

Her mother's eyes swam with tears. "Then it will be our blood that flows."

"Good day to you, mother. May our next meeting hold more joy." Rahab offered a brief salute and turned, walking away. Tears dripped, one cheek still stinging from her mother's touch. How would she convince them now? She would be three days in the tents.

Israelites: None slept easy that night. Salmon ate a piece of manna, but the pit in his stomach did not want food. "Be not afraid". He repeated the words periodically. This was a good thing to be doing. A way to separate themselves from the heathens in their land.

The sound of trumpets announced the time had come. Salmon was glad, better for the experience to pass, then to be waiting in fear for it. He lined up with the others. As time passed, his heart thudded. Deep cries of men whistled through the wind.

"Why do the men cry?" Elimelech pressed against Salmon's side.

Though anxiety clenched his throat, he leaned down and explained the process of circumcision.

Elimelech blanched. Salmon's firm hold on his thin shoulder kept the boy from running. "We are YHWH's people. This act of obedience will reward us in the end."

His own words mocked the pain lancing through him as the afternoon wore on. He moved cautiously to the table and set his focus on the parchment. Bezrah, seated across from him, added lines to their map of Jericho. "Your attention to detail is thorough. I had forgotten much of what you've drawn." Salmon tapped a northern section of the wall. "Rahab's inn?"

Bezrah nodded. "The palace and temple were easy to see, don't know what lies beyond."

"We have what we need." Joshua entered the tent. Salmon rushed to stand, then moaned as pain gripped his groin.

Joshua held his hand up, insisting they remain seated. "Now is the time for healing." He lounged near them, using a cushion on the ground.

"Your pain does not seem great." Bezrah observed with a wince.

Joshua offered a smile. "My circumcision took place shortly after the exodus from Egypt. My sympathy for your pain remains. Tell me of the Canaanite woman."

Bezrah offered Salmon a smirk. "I understood none of her words. She is Salmon's to explain."

"We met her at the well after entering with a small group of merchants. Far fewer travelers than I expected. She offered us a break of fast, then said it would be wise to remove ourselves from the street. She has a strange painted face, but her eyes are kind. I'm not sure how she knew, but she did." Salmon studied Joshua, wondering what the leader thought of his ramblings. The look in Joshua's gray eyes bade him continue. He cleared his throat. "She gave us strange food, meat for one. Not of a swine."

Joshua smiled. "Not bird?"

"There were vegetables as well. And a strange yellow food that seemed almost like it had rolled around in a pan."

Bezrah interrupted. "Don't forget the cushions. Bright fabrics stuffed with something that made them soft. We sat on them."

"There are strange things you have yet to encounter." Joshua pointed at the map they had drawn. "One day you may have houses of your own, not desert tents."

Bezrah shrugged. "To be cut off from the sun? From the wind?"

"There are many battles to be won before you need make a choice." Joshua returned his attention to Salmon. "What made you promise the woman her life?"

"Soldiers entered the streets looking for us. She saw them. We thought to climb over the wall at that time, but she bade us wait. We would easily be captured in the light of day. Instead, she hid us beneath plants set to dry on the roof of her house. After night fell, she brought us back into the house. She showed us the mountains in the north. Bid us wait there."

"Why wait?"

"A band of soldiers left Jericho in search of us. She told the king we had snuck out and were returning to our land in the east. He sent them after us."

"She lied?"

"What other way does she know? She has not

learned to hold sacred the things of our way. And yet, YWHW reached out for her."

Joshua's brows lifted. "She spoke his name?"

"She called Him our God. YWHW has caused the people of Jericho to tremble with fear. She asked that we might save her and her family alive in return for her kindness to us. I felt no caution in my spirit, and I promised."

Joshua tugged on his beard, allowing a moment of contemplation. Salmon could read nothing, no sense of approval or discontent with Salmon's choice. The older man finally offered a grin. "I would not expect redeeming from that which is already condemned for destruction."

"The Lord has delivered them into our hands. They tremble with fear, even I could tell, though I speak not their language." Bezrah added, then grimaced as he shifted too much.

"And what think you of the woman?"

"She fears our Lord more than the king of her city."

Joshua stood. "Remain as you are, be well. We will linger a few days for healing."

"What of Rahab and her family?" Salmon asked, uncertain why his heart beat stronger in his chest.

"YHWH prepares a place for them. Who am I to stand in His way?"

The Fourteenth Day of the Month of Abib
Within Jericho:

Rahab leaned against a pillow as clouds of smoke wafted through the air. The heavy scent of herbs kept her thoughts spinning. How many days had it been since she'd entered the blood tent? She shook her head and glanced at the cloths beneath her. Red cloths. Her cycle had never been like this. The incense tub at the center of the tent belched another cloud of smoke. What were they burning?

This wasn't usual. Rahab rubbed her eyes. Something needed to be done, something important, but her mind didn't want to focus. Lingering in this place was dangerous, but why? Silhouettes of two women at the opening of the tent, backlit by sunlight, caught her attention. They must be the tenders, there to help. Rahab stumbled as she pushed herself to her feet. She gathered the filthy rags and made her way to the opening.

"Dark days," an old woman grumbled.

"It's sunny." Rahab sighed as she felt the touch of fresh air caress her cheek.

"Should be dark as the hearts of the cursed army," the other elder muttered as she snatched Rahab's soiled towels and handed her fresh ones.

The Israelites were not a cursed army. The sweet smell of spring air drove the fog from her mind. Rahab dipped a clean cloth in a vat of clear water. She moved to the back of the tent, past the other woman moaning in her spot on the floor, to the ripped canvas. She cleaned herself as best she could with the wet cloth, then sank to the ground in a space where fresh air from the break in the tent countered the heady effects of whatever had been added to the smoke.

It helped. She leaned back and dozed. What were the Israelites doing? Had her two spies returned safely to them?

Israelites: Rashid, Salmon, Sepher, and Elimelech stood with Meishal at the Judean corral. Rashid pointed, jabbing Salmon's arm. "That one. The lamb has the whitest coat; I see no blemish."

Lambs were dumb like their parents, and it didn't take much effort to catch the one selected by the youngest son. Rashid held the lamb by its hooves and carried it across his neck.

"This will be a fine sacrifice." Salmon watched others of the tribe of Judah grabbing their lambs for the Passover, then he returned his attention to his family crossing the camp.

During the time of healing from circumcision, the Tabernacle had been raised. The Tabernacle marked the center of the camp. Each tribe had an assigned position to the north, east, west, and south. The tribe of Judah was to the east. They approached the crowded gate into the Tabernacle. Salmon remained with the others. Very little talk passed between any of them. Though Salmon tried to keep his thoughts on the purpose of Passover, going through the plagues of Egypt in his mind, he couldn't help but wonder what was happening in the city of Jericho, far beyond their eastern camp.

When the blood had been spilled from the lamb, Rashid returned the carcass to his shoulders, and the procession followed Meishal to the tents in their area of the camp. Mother and Elia had prepared a pit, red hot coals lining where the meat would roast. It did not take long to skin the lamb, and soon they laid it on the flat stone above the coals. Fires tended on either side of the roast fed the coals, keeping the roaster hot enough to cook the meat.

The scent of roasting meat wafted across the plains of Jericho. As evening drew near, the moon rose like a giant orb beyond the Jordan River. Salmon latched the top hook of his tunic as he stood in the opening of his tent, watching the full moon. Had it shone as bright on the original Passover? The cloud of YHWH remained firmly in place over the Holy of Holies. How could any choose to worship the moon, distant and unreachable, when YHWH Creator remained present with them?

The opening songs drew Salmon from his strange wonderings. Sounds of worship rose throughout the camp of Israel as they celebrated Passover for the first time inside the Promise Land.

Within Jericho: Fresher air proved healthful. With a pause in her cycle, and a deep hunger for a meal, Rahab slipped from the tent without notice. She wrapped her dark cloak around herself and stayed close to the buildings, using shadows as she could.

Home was not far from the tents. The inn was empty. It shouldn't be, she paid a caretaker to watch when she was away. No harm had been done. She pulled potatoes from the cellar, along with a slab of smoked fish. She didn't smell anything distinctive, indicating the fish had spoiled. Of course, that could be from the powerful herbs used in the tent. She frowned, setting fire to the coals so she could cook her meal. She couldn't risk more than a few hours away.

There was singing carried on the wind as the moon rose above Jericho. Rahab sat in her window looking over the wall into the plains of Jericho. The flicker of campfire flames in the dark made it seem as though fire raged across the land. Fire coming to cleanse them. Soldiers paced from one garrison to the other, the sound of their boots clanking on stone. But still, she could hear something, a language she did not understand.

Would she learn to speak their language? Would they be allowed to stay with the Israelites? Salmon and she hadn't discussed specifics. She chewed on her bottom lip as her belly cramped. She needed to return to the blood tents. With darkness fallen, she could easily sneak in without the tending women noticing.

She wrapped her cloak around herself and slipped into the night. The tents were not far from the inn, set between the gates as a compromise for those women who did not wish to travel beyond the walls. Women experiencing their monthly cycle would spend three days in prayers within the tents. Sensors within burned incense pleasing to the gods as the women sat upon rags. When the rags became blood-soaked, the tending women would soak them in water and then set them out to dry so they could be reused. The blood red water was taken to the pools at the temple.

Rahab listened a moment for the anxious voices of

the tenders. She slipped through a back opening and took her place. One other woman sat in the tent, her body weaving back and forth. Rahab coughed in the haze. Her mind whirled. Rather than fight against it, she settled on her rags and leaned back to sleep.

The Fifteenth Day of the Month of Abib
Israelites:

Salmon stretched, pleased to feel no pain.
He straightened his sleeping mat and grabbed the basket sitting outside. None other of his family had risen. Manna lay on the ground, ready to gather. He put enough for his family in the basket and carried it back to their area. It wasn't long before they were all sitting around a fire to eat. "Bezrah and others are going to gather crops. I'd like to go with them." Salmon looked at Meishal. Even at twenty-six, it was proper to gain permission from the elder.

"From where?" Bilhah looked around.

"Further south of the camp there are farms that have been deserted, their food is going to spoil. No need for that."

Meishal broke manna. "We can have a proper feast. Bring what you can for unleavened bread."

A great number of them went, more and more as they realized the bounty that was available. By noon of the day, bread sizzled in pans. Salmon and Sepher argued over which vegetables could be roasted with the bread. Salmon did not know the name of most of them. Would Rahab be able to help with that?

The noon meal proved filling, and Salmon sat in the opening of his tent, as others were doing. Meishal slept. His own eyes drifted closed, but he blinked them open. His part was to watch, let the others take their rest. The air around him shimmered, the wind not a true sound, and yet, he could hear it. The noise of the camp faded away. Not far to the east, Joshua strode toward someone. The stranger, even if his sword had not been drawn, would have seemed larger, white robes brighter than the clouds dotting the blue sky. Joshua fell to his knees. Salmon tried to watch, but his eyes wearied, closed. It wasn't until the piercing blow of a trumpet had him jumping to his feet, vision gone. No man, no stranger. The second sounding of the trumpet called for soldiers to meet at the gathering place.

"I have met with the Lord and we have a battle plan unlike any other." Joshua stood on a raised platform of rock. Thousands gathered, and yet his voice rose strong and clear for all to hear. "The ark will go with us; seven priests shall trumpet before the ark. The armed guard will go in front of the ark and the rear guard will follow it. We walk the wall of Jericho one time today. The only sound of your passing will be that of the priests. No cries of your own, no word shall you speak, whatever you may see as we travel around the city. You will remain silent in the march until the day I tell you to make a mighty shout. On that day, Jericho will be ours."

A shout rose among the soldiers, and then silence as they prepared to do as Joshua bid. Salmon tapped spears with Bezrah as they joined the formation.

Within Jericho: "They've come. Silent as ghosts, they've come!" The tender's cry made Rahab's stomach drop. She wasn't at the inn. Surely something within would urge her to return to her home. Salmon had warned that none without would be spared. She slipped through the rear of the blood tents once more and made her way home.

She did not need to step through her window and onto the wall to see the odd procession. Beyond the reach of arrows, Israelite soldiers marched twelve men deep in a line that seemed to go forever. Thousands of them, and yet the only sound was the faint shriek of trumpets. The sound grew louder, and Rahab could see the men blowing trumpets. They wore long robes, not armor. As did the four behind them carrying a great box. Its golden hue shone in the sunlight and she could not bear to look. She sank to her knees beside the window. The warmth of *I am*, who met her in her dreams, washed over her now. Surely their God was with them.

It took an hour for the line to go beyond her sight from the north-facing window. Rahab waited, her head against the cold stone as she sat on the floor, expecting the sound of battle. The day had nearly waned when shocked voices spoke nearby.

"They returned to their camp."

Rahab leaned through the window. "What do you mean?"

A soldier she did not know shrugged. "They walked the perimeter of the city and now return to their camp."

"But why?"

None could answer her. Rahab returned for her

final night in the blood tents. What were the Israelites doing?

The Sixteenth Day of the Month of Abib

"It is not a Sabbath, is it?" Rashid pushed against Salmon who still lay on his mat.

Salmon hit back. "What?"

"YHWH does not send manna on the Sabbath."

Salmon groaned, wanting to sleep a bit longer. "Correct. Sabbath was two nights past when we celebrated Passover."

"But there is no manna today."

"What do you mean?" No manna? Week after week, year after year for his entire life, manna fell with the dawn and birds came at supper. "You are mistaken." Salmon pushed himself to his feet, but from the noise beyond his tent opening, something had happened. He and Rashid went outside as Bilhah held up a basket.

"We can eat what you gathered from the land yesterday." She shrugged, gazing into the full basket.

Salmon took it from her to carry to the fire pit between her and Meishal's tent. "Use the grains to make bread? I can help Elia cut open these plants, perhaps we find something useful."

"You are a good son. I can see why Joshua picked you. Elia's friend, Anna, will be here this afternoon. You should think on her."

"Anna? She is too young."

"She is a woman, and you are a man in need of a wife."

A different woman came unbidden to mind. The likes of Rahab were forbidden. He turned his thoughts to the provision of YHWH. "Now is a time for war, not romance. I promise to seek a wife when the season is right."

Bilhah sighed, then gave him a warm smile. "You are a good son; I will trust your judgement."

Would she be so quick to think so, if she knew the first woman to gain his attention painted her eyes and had not crossed desert sands with them? He rubbed the back of his neck. When the time was right, his heart would open to a good Israeli girl, as was meant to happen for a prince of Judah.

He gave Bilhah the grains necessary to make bread, then lifted the basket. "Elia," he hollered as he crossed to her section of camp.

It was different, but sufficient. Salmon licked his fingers. "We can gather more supplies today."

"Is there to be nothing more from YHWH?" Rashid's eyes grew round with worry.

Meishal smiled. "He has brought us to lands flowing with milk and honey. We are no longer wanderers in the desert."

"YHWH be praised." Bilhah squeezed his hand.

Trumpets called. Meishal clasped Sepher and Salmon. "Let us hear the plan for today."

"Salmon." Joshua waved him over as the troops prepared for a second day's procession.

Salmon jogged to him. "Sir?" Joshua's eyes shone with strength. Not even the strange directions to walk the city had any impact on his demeanor.

"When we return, gather tents that can be used for the Jerichobite and her family. Find a space beyond the tribes, but still within distance of camp."

"Should they not be among us?"

Joshua shook his head. "Not at first. I await the Lord's instruction."

"Very well." Salmon nodded. He looked across the valley as Joshua turned away and went about his business. A place he could have an excuse to go near them. The collection center for the eastern side of the Tabernacle could work. Not right there, the waste would stink, but close. He pulled his fingers through his short beard. It could work.

"Are you joining us today?" Bezrah's knock against his shoulder jarred Salmon from his thoughts.

He struck Bezrah with the wood of his spear.

Bezrah groaned, grabbing his shoulder. "Wound me this near to your tents and I'll have your sister Elia tend to me."

Salmon laughed. "She's more likely to hit your other side."

Bezrah wagged his brows. "A feisty one, I think I'll like her all the more."

Salmon rolled his eyes, pulling his friend toward the gathering army. "We have a battle more likely to be won."

The wall of Jericho loomed above them. The inner rank of the army kept shields raised to ward off arrows, should any make it this far. Salmon matched his steps with the others in his row and with the soldiers before him. They raised right foot then left in unison. The march took them past the gate for the Eastern road. It had been sealed shut. The dismantled ramp formed a heap at the base of the wall. There were windows in the wall. They must be places like Rahab. A few faces watched them from the shadows.

The sun had not peaked overhead so the air around them remained refreshed with a cool touch. Step after step they marched in procession, and above the sounds of leather creaking, the rattle of shields, the thud of foot after foot striking the ground, above all that, Salmon heard the jaunts of the inhabitants of Jericho. Gawkers stood on top of the wall. "Dogs." "Miscreants." "Ghosts." He understood the words floating around them as few others could. But it didn't take knowing the language to hear the fear in their voices, the terror in their shouts.

Something floated in the wind, a crimson cord tied to a window close to one of the garrisons. Rahab's inn. He could still see plants drying on her roof. What did she think as they marched past?

The Seventeenth Day of the Month of Abib

"Mother." Rahab sat straighter as she recognized the woman entering the bleeding tent. "Your seasons have passed the time of blood. What do you mean, joining us?" She slid a glance at the woman across from her. The other's attention did not stir.

Malicha sat beside her on the rags. She leaned close, gripping Rahab's arm. "The gods do nothing against Jewish dogs. Hour after hour they burn up children." Her body shook. "The boys... I tried to take them west of the city, but soldiers bar the gates. They will come for them, Rahab. They will take them and burn them on the fires in the temple." Her voice choked as she pressed her head against Rahab's shoulder.

Rahab gripped her mother's hand. "Have them hide in the cart. Load your clothes over them and take the cart to the inn. We will hide them there."

"Death waits, whether it is within or without."

"There is hope. To the inn. My cycle should cease within the day. I will meet you there. If the need arises, take them to the roof. Have them hide beneath the flax. Give them Valerian root. They will sleep."

Cramps clenched her insides. She blew breath through her lips as she watched Malicha leave the room. She closed her eyes. *You promised my family.*

May they arrive safely. But what of her sisters? Neither had yet to heed her warning. She carried her soiled rags to the tending woman and returned with clean. Sight of the blood-red water turned her stomach. What happened in the temple? Drums beat. She pressed her hands against her ears, but the sound moved through the floor, throbbed in her chest.

The quiet of the blood sanctuary shattered as the reed door struck the inside wall. A priest walked past the soldier. The wild look in his eyes made her body cold. Specks of blood marred his white-painted face. The woman across from her moaned. He pushed her aside, dug beneath the pile of rags. The woman clawed uselessly at his arm as he raised an infant above his head. A soldier knocked her down, but it didn't stop the woman from clambering after them. Her shrieks from the street beyond the sanctuary silenced. Rahab held her breath. Was there naught that could stay the madness?

The Eighteenth Day of the Month of Abib

A different sort of drumming moved through her as she crossed the inner gate toward the inn. Her blood cycle had mostly ended, but she needed to remove herself as far as she could from the temple. The ground trembled. She lifted her skirts and ran for home.

The space between the walls filled with people. Shouts clamored from the walkway on the wall. Musicians played in the street, encouraging dancers to jostle the crowd. Rahab pushed her way through to the inn. The arch into her garden lay in pieces, thick rocks tumbled on the ground between the two sides that remained standing. Plants had been trampled underfoot. The water skin had a gash. Heart thumping, she sprinted across the pathway into her home.

But inside was quiet. The madness without had not made its way beyond the front garden.

"Mother? Father?" she hollered. The ground vibrated through her sandals. They were too far from the temple to hear drums. She raced up the stairs, taking them two at a time.

Sentries stood on either side of the window; she could see their bronzed legs. Beyond them, just beyond the reach of Jericho, the army of Israel marched. Row upon row, numbers she hadn't imagined made their way around.

"What are they doing?" Rahab stared through the window. As far as she could see, they marched. Silent in voice, but the thrum of their steps jumbled the ground within the walls.

Malicha grabbed her arm. "It is the third day. Once around, quiet as ghosts. It isn't natural."

Rahab watched a moment longer, then turned to her mother, offering a brief hug. "Remain inside. Are father and the boys here?"

"They are. What do you expect to happen? Here or in the streets, our doom awaits."

"Not for us." Rahab glanced through the window. "Not if we obey."

"Why? What have you done?"

Rahab took Malicha's hands. "I offered aid. In return, they gave a promise."

Her mother's eyes darkened. "How can you trust the words of dogs?"

"We are the dogs. I have every reason to hope in their words. I tried to convince Rebacca and Richelle to come as well," she shook her head, "but they will not heed my warning."

"Wicked girl." She tried to pull her hands away. "You dishonor our name."

Rahab refused to let her go. "Why will you not sacrifice the boys? Blood has flowed for weeks at the temple, and yet the children of Israel march beyond the wall. There is no power in the gods of Jericho. We have been deceived. The living God of Israel will crush us beneath the feet of his people. If any are to be feared, surely Israel's God!"

Malicha's cheeks dampened with tears. "I don't

know what to think."

"Let the signs and wonders provide your evidence. What we have heard. What we see today and will see in the days to come."

"I fear for our lives."

Rahab hugged her mother. "We have less to fear than any other in Jericho."

The Twenty-first Day of the Month of Abib

Seven days they came, marching like silent ghosts, impervious to the insults and debris shot at them. Rahab crouched beside her window. Jericho was almost in a frenzy with panic. They would kill themselves from the inside out. Perhaps that was the intent of the Jews.

A scream sounded from the front of the inn. A familiar scream that caused Rahab to leap from her place by the window. She raced down the stairs and out the door. One of the twins struggled against Captain Axard. His steel eyes glinted as he held the boy and stared at her. Rahab didn't think. She grabbed the walking stick beside the door and ran to protect her brother. Dog growled beside her.

She swung the stick, curling it over her head as one of her patrons had demonstrated, and struck the captain in his arm. With a hiss, he released Leti. The boy fell to the ground and Rahab waved him out of the way. He ran behind her. Blood smeared his lip, but she didn't have time to wonder. Captain Axard grabbed the stick. He broke it and tossed the ends into the street.

Dog lurched between them. Captain Axard kicked it. Rahab screamed and Leti ran to the dog. The captain pushed Rahab against the wall. Two smaller bodies rammed into them, and dogs barked.

"Get your filthy hands off our sister."

Captain Axard threw a punch toward one of them, but the boy ducked.

Rahab grabbed his arm. "Let them be." She struggled to keep him from them as two dogs jumped and snarled.

Dassub's voice boomed across the garden. "Your place is not here, Captain." The dogs ran to his side.

The captain held her fast, though she struggled against him. "What business is it to you, old man. Your daughter is a whore."

"Your place is on the ramparts. They have come around again."

"What?" He did not loosen his grip on Rahab as he turned to glare at Dassub.

"The enemy have started a second tour of Jericho."

Captain Axard's grip loosened and Rahab pushed herself from his clutches.

"The silent march has not returned to camp." Dassub stepped beside her. "They are circling our city a second time."

Rahab held her two brothers as captain snarled, pointing in their direction. "It is a day for blood. Yours will flow as easily as the others."

"Return to your duty, sir. Jericho has need of you."

Captain removed himself from Rahab's front garden. Rahab, weak kneed, looked to her father, but remained unable to read him.

He shook his head. "Your sisters have made good matches. Why refuse such a man yourself?"

"A strong captain does not have the makings of a good match. One cannot love with one breath and war with another." Rahab breathed as Dog sat beside her. She rubbed its head. The other dog yapped at Leti and Arron. Rahab glanced at the open door of the inn. "Is Mother here? Where are my sisters? Have they not arrived yet?"

"Their husbands refuse to come. They say there will be no need to flee."

"But they must be here. I cannot protect them if they are not in the house."

"How would you protect them? You could not prevent the captain harming you."

What could she do? Today would be the day. The Israelites marched a second time around the city. Could she risk being caught outside the house? If her sisters remained with the men they chose, their lodgings would be the first street after the inner gate. An hour there and back. Was it possible?

"Remain here, inside the house." Rahab pushed the twins to her father. "Keep them hidden. Captain Axard may return to try to take them to the priests."

"Where are you going?"

"To convince my sisters this is the best place for them." Rahab paused as Dog made to follow her. She pointed at the door of the inn. "Stay. Watch over the boys." Surprisingly, the dog obeyed, chasing the smaller animal who followed the twins into the inn. Her heart tightened in her chest. She had to find Richelle and Rebacca.

She ran through the streets crowded with people heading for the walls. They wanted to see their enemies. *What if Richelle and Rebacca aren't in their homes? What if they've come to the wall?* Rahab searched the sea of people. She grabbed a familiar woman from the market. "Do you know Rebacca? Have you seen her?"

The woman pushed her away. Rahab ran on. An hour later, she'd returned to the wall, searching the crowds of people standing in the way. Shouts to the soldiers on the walls resulted in updates. Rahab pushed herself through the maddening crowd. Ahead, she noticed a familiar sweep of hair. Rahab darted between an older couple arguing. She tripped but managed to grab hold of Richelle. Richelle's eyes danced, the smell of drink strong on her breath.

She grabbed Rahab with an excited squeal. "Have you seen them? Round and round they go. I don't know what they expect." Rahab hugged sister, but Richelle pushed her away. "What is wrong with you?"

"Come to my house. You will be able to see over the wall."

"Zuni has been stationed here." She looked up at the wall and waved at a man. Rahab couldn't tell if it was sister's husband or another man. "He asked me to watch for him. Wants me to witness his splendor in battle."

"You are not safe here. Neither is Rebacca. Wait for the battle in my home."

Richelle pushed her away. "Go hide, little sister." She laughed as Rahab tripped over a table of baskets. "These walls are strong. Have you seen anything of this foreign army that could bring it down? What have we to fear?"

Clouds were gathering, and a wind across the city brought the stench of rot. Too many sacrifices to consume on the fires. Whatever the Jews planned would happen this day. Soon, their God would destroy

Jericho. Rahab looked at her sister one last time. "Please."

Richelle turned away. Rahab twisted to crawl from the baskets. Someone grabbed her hair and pulled her to her feet. Captain Axard pulled her close. "My men and I searched three days for those spies, until enemy movement forced us to return. Are they still here? Your spies? Do they plan to open the gates somehow?" Captain Axard snarled and a bit of spittle dripped on Rahab's cheek.

She turned, trying to twist free. "There are no spies in Jericho. Shouldn't you be on the wall with your men?"

He released his hold on her and slammed the back of his hand across her face. "You mean to tell me my business?"

Rahab staggered back but managed to stay on her feet. Excited villagers pushed between them. She turned and fled. It didn't matter if he followed or not, the need to reach her home burned in her chest. She turned the corner and the remains of the arch of her garden came into view. She ran between the stones.

"Rahab." The captain's voice thundered. She didn't dare turn to look as she stumbled on the walkway leading up to the main entrance into the inn. The sound of trumpets burst forth as she crossed the threshold. Like thunder, the trumpet sound rumbled, growing louder until the ground beneath their feet moved with the force of it.

Rahab stood in the doorway as the world outside the inn rose and fell. She turned and saw Captain Axard drop to his knees.

"Don't watch, Rahab."

She flung herself around. "Salmon." She stumbled into him as the ground shook.

"Your face," his thumb touched skin close to her eye. Pain twinged across her brow. She winced.

He pulled her forward. "Come. We can leave by the upper window. We've taken your family already."

"But not my sisters."

"I am sorry, Rahab. They would have to be here to be saved."

She let him lead her up the stairs but pulled to the side to grab her bag. She slung it over her shoulder and wrapped it around her body. The air around them rumbled with battle. The sight from her place on the wall took her breath. The walls of Jericho had fallen in on themselves. Rocks broken like a child's toy had fallen against the inner wall. All the outer wall lay crumbled, except where her house stood. The entire wall in either direction... impossible... improbable. Darkness swam across her consciousness and she fell into it.

"Rahab." Salmon caught her before she hit the ground. Though he'd helped with his younger sister, touching a woman was foreign to him. How was he to carry her down the wall? The stairs had been there for the others. He slung her body over his shoulder, grateful her thick skirts prevented any truly indecent touching. He grabbed hold of the red rope hanging from the casement.

His hand burned as he held the woman and lowered them both safely to the ground. Screams of battle raged behind him as he jogged toward the river. He curtailed the main camp, turning north to the site he'd selected for the heathens.

Rahab moved against his shoulder. Her moan whispered against his body. He paused, crouching to lay her on the ground. Her eyes blinked open, deep golden eyes that slanted differently than his own people. He put the thought aside as she struggled to sit up. He did not offer to assist.

"What happened?" She looked at a copse of trees near a creek that crossed the valley until it reached the Jordan River.

"You fainted. I brought you from Jericho, as promised." He pointed to a group of tents that had been set up.

She searched the barren grasslands. "But my family…"

"A site has been prepared for you in our camp."

Her brows rose. "With you? You mean us to be slaves? Would it not have been better to let us die with our own people?"

He pressed his finger against her lips. The act surprised them both. "There is not intent to harm. Your lives have been spared for sparing ours."

"Should you not send us elsewhere?"

"Where would you go? War controls this land. The God of Abraham, Isaac, and Jacob directs war against all the inhabitants that would stand against us. You are safest here."

"But what will happen? We are not of your people."

"I do not know the plans God has for you. I do know His hand was upon your house while the wall crumbled and fell." Was it possible? Salmon watched as she blinked tears from her eyes. Strength and determination set in her face. How was it no other woman in his tribe caused him to notice such detail? She was a heathen. He had no place noticing anything about her. He stood, offering his hand to help her to her feet.

But he'd forgotten the burning of the rope. He hissed as she gripped his hand.

With her feet on the ground, Rahab turned his hand over. "You hurt yourself."

Angry red welts cut across his palm and the back of his hand. "From the rope I used to climb down the wall. It will heal."

"Aloe will help." She dug into the bag slung around her shoulder and pulled a small wooden box from inside. She slid the lid open and dug salve from the box. She spread it across both sides of his hand.

The sting dulled, and he found he could flex his fingers. "That helps." Her kindness touched his heart. That wasn't right, was it? "We should continue. Your family will be anxious to know you are safe." He paused, then felt compelled to offer appreciation. "Thank you."

Her lips twitched up in a semblance of a smile as she returned the box to her bag. They continued across the field to the tents.

The scent of blood washed away in the waters of the Jordan. Salmon let the gentle waves brush against his hands. He had killed, and yet the memory of battle remained hazy. Though the sun set far to the west, the blaze of the city on fire filled the sky with light and smoke. He stepped out of the water, jerking his head back and forth to shake off droplets of wet.

Other soldiers surrounded him, though he did not know any well. He lifted his gear and joined them on the march returning to camp.

"God bless you this day." A younger man from the tribe of Benjamin stepped closer.

Salmon recognized the marks on the armor. "May His breath be ever at your back."

"You brought several from Jericho to tents pitched north of here." The young man's tone alluded more to curiosity than vengeance.

"Yes, with Joshua's blessing and the hand of our Lord."

"Do you think they know cooking? Something they could teach our wives? Do they have supplies?"

Help with cooking, now that manna and daily birds no longer fell to them, had come to mind. But supplies? Salmon looked at the burning city. There had been packages, bags of clothing, and personal items, he was sure. But enough? He hadn't even considered sleeping mats for the tents.

The Twenty-second Day of the Month of Abib

Rahab watched Malicha shiver beneath a
thin blanket, whether from fear or chill she could not
tell.

"They will pack us here like chattel." Malicha
faced the direction of the Israel camp, visible from a
distance.

Rahab removed her coat and wrapped it around her
mother. "There are no others coming from Jericho."

"How do you know?"

"Their God warned our people to leave Jericho.
We had an opportunity to remove ourselves from the
land of Canaan, but we refused."

"And why shouldn't we?"

"You told the story many times when I was young.
The great Jacob and his sons leaving, with a promise to
return one day." She looked across the innumerable
tents scattered throughout the lands. "They have come."

A familiar man drew near, his hand on the harness
of a mule pulling a cart.

Malicha noticed Rahab's attention and turned to
look. "He is one who led us from the inn."

"His name is Salmon. He is one of the two men I
hid."

"Why did they spare us if none of the others?"

Rahab picked beneath her nails. She dreaded the question yet knew Malicha needed the truth. "Several weeks ago, two men entered through the gates. Their look was different than any other. I knew if they were discovered they would be tortured and killed. I chose to hide them instead." She took a breath. "I helped them leave when night fell."

Her mother sucked in air. "Why would you do such things?"

"They needed to be done."

"How can you speak thus?"

"I've been dreaming of their God. I say their God," she looked across the sea of tents, then settled her eyes on Salmon. "Yet, I sense all creatures may belong to him. If there were a god above all gods, surely He would be."

Malicha shook her head. "I do not understand."

Rahab looked at her mother. "Neither do I, but the city burns and here we are."

Salmon's donkey slowed to a stop and he moved near enough for a greeting. "Shalom. I know you do not have much. I brought supplies." He lifted a blanket and walked to Malicha, wrapping it around her.

Confusion rolled through Rahab at the act of kindness. Supplies indeed. He and his men unloaded bedding, blankets, food, clothing, pottery, and utensils. Rahab traced her finger along a blue line etched in a water pot. "This is a royal color. Is it so common to your people?" She glanced at Salmon. He flushed, and a horrid thought twisted the nerves in her belly. "You are royal."

He shrugged. "Of the tribe of Judah."

"How many tribes are there?"

"Twelve." He placed a table inside the larger tent.

Leti and Arron peeked through the opening of another tent. Their attention moved from Salmon to the donkey. Rahab waved them back inside when they moved in the direction of the animal. She bowed at Salmon. "I am sorry, Prince. I did not know."

He rubbed his neck and cast a glance at his men. "None of that, if you will."

"I do not understand."

"My family position has no bearing. I am a soldier."

"With a kingly heart. Thank you for this."

"It is my pleasure."

Rahab smiled. "I'm surprised you did not build our shelters with plants. The day you spent beneath them could not have been comfortable."

"The king's palace would have been far worse. I will bring more provisions tomorrow. Let me know if you have need."

She nodded, wrapping her arms around herself as he stepped away. Odd feelings moved within, familiar and yet strange.

Salmon released his men and led the donkey to the stall. Horse shook his head, ignoring the lesser animal, yet seeking attention from Salmon as he turned to leave. Salmon nuzzled the great beast's head. "I know a pair of lads that would be interested in meeting you. Perhaps if you promise not to harm either of them, I will take you with me tomorrow."

"I can only hope the animal will reply to you one day. I hope I am there to see you jump back in astonishment."

Salmon greeted his brother, Sepher. "You don't usually travel this close to horses. What do you want?"

"Not me. Mother. She heard you were near and wanted word of the battle."

"I could use a good meal."

"A wife could help with that, if you chose the proper one."

An image of Rahab at the fire interrupted his thoughts. He swept them away. "My time is for battle, for now. It will not always be thus, Lord willing."

"Why are you here?"

"We have inhabitants brought from Jericho. I knew they needed supplies."

"Prisoners? Joshua forbid saving any of that accursed city."

"These were sanctioned. You may check for yourself, I have no desire to bring shame upon us."

Sepher lowered his head. "I mean no disrespect."

"None taken. If you were to know and do nothing, God's curse would surely fall upon us all."

Twenty-third Day of the Month of Abib

Morning, the second after the fall of Jericho. Rahab stirred a pot of oats and milk boiling on the fire as hooves sounded across the ground. The twins, followed by two dogs, ran through the opening of their tent as Salmon entered the camp. Rahab jumped to her feet, holding her hand out as though she could grab the boys from a distance.

Salmon smiled at her and winked. Never mind it caused flutters in her belly. She watched the twins grab hold of each other and halt a few steps from the giant beast. The dogs knew no such caution. They scooted closer, sniffing at the hoofs of the great beast. The horse leaned down and blew. The dogs scattered. Salmon held a rein in one hand and patted the horse with his other. It bumped its head against his shoulder. Curious, Rahab stepped closer.

"This is Horse."

"Of course, we know what it is." The boys laughed. "What did you name it?"

"Horse."

Rahab laughed at the confused look on twin faces. "Not creative, are you?"

Arron tilted his head. "You named your horse, Horse?"

"Nothing else seemed to work."

"Can we pet him?" Leti took a step closer, his face bright with anticipation.

Salmon held up his hand. "This, first." He gave a push and Horse turned, its head moving closer to the twins. "Hold your hands where he can smell you."

They giggled. "Smell us?" The smaller of the two raised his hand beneath the nostrils of the horse. A snort dropped horse snot across his fingers and Leti squealed.

Salmon laughed. "He likes you."

Not to be outdone by his younger twin, Arron moved his hand closer as well, bumping into the horse. Horse didn't seem impressed and jerked its head up and down. Arron snatched his hand back.

"Whoa, now. That wasn't a proper greeting, Horse." Salmon nuzzled the large animal. "Give the boy a proper greeting."

Arron didn't seem to want to hold his hand for inspection yet again, and Rahab moved closer. But Horse stretched its neck and nuzzled Arron against his shoulder.

"He likes you as well," Salmon announced with pride. "Come this way, you can rub your hand on his side." He drew the boys closer to himself, showing them where they could rub their hands against the horse's side. He grinned at Rahab. "Would you like to meet Horse as well?"

The animal was warm beneath her hand, its coarse hair tickling her skin. Salmon's hand remained close to hers without touching. His eyes were a mystery, yet he laughed when he turned to the twins.

"Next time I'll bring his brush. Teach you how to groom him."

Leti widened his eyes. "Horse has his hair brushed?"

"He will need it when we head north, to Ai."

The boys leaned closer with excitement. "You go to battle?"

He nodded. "Our leader, Joshua, has sent a troop to spy it out for us."

Rahab grinned. "He didn't want to send you this time?"

Salmon's eyes sparked. "I couldn't possibly outdo my first job as spy."

Rahab pressed her forehead against the horse for a moment, taking in the rush of feeling before allowing her mind to admit the folly of it. When she looked up, Salmon's attention had turned to the twins.

Sixth Day of the Month of Iyar

Rahab glanced across the tent at the soft gleam of morning light coming through the opening. How many days had they been with the Jews? With? She closed her eyes. Apart. Oh, they came. Not close enough to meet, to give ear to the strange language that seemed to come from them. They came to glare with cold eyes. His short visits with supplies broke the monotony of her day. Salmon. She closed her eyes. Fruitless to think on him, and yet... She sighed. Fires needed tending. Breakfast to be prepared. Rahab threw the blankets from her cot with a grunt.

Grains boiled in water. Rahab added a pinch of salt as her mother ran closer.

Malicha wrenched her hands, looking across the valley. "What is this great noise?"

Rahab stood. An odd noise, like weeping, swept across the area. She shaded her eyes and looked across the camp. She saw movement but could not tell why. The strange noise crescendoed into thousands of tongues crying beneath the morning sky. Rahab wrapped her arm around her mother's shoulders. "I will go. It sounds as though tragedy has fallen on them."

The twins jumped in the opening of their tent. "And us?" Leti widened his eyes with hope. The pair of dogs pressed between them.

Rahab grinned, walking closer to the boys with her mother. Rahab ruffled their hair, though they ducked to get away. "Not this morn," she told them. "You will come another time. It will be good for you to move through the Israel camp."

"They sound funny." Arron nodded his head.

Leti made a face. "Use words that don't make sense."

A deeper voice joined the conversation. "When have you heard them speak?" Dassub's voice boomed. The twins scraped their toes in the dirt. He gave them a hard look then faced Rahab. "I will be certain they remain here. Be careful, daughter."

Rahab nabbed a shawl, covering her head and wrapping her shoulders to ward off the touch of chill in the morning air. Sound of crying and warbling voices filled the valley. Language she did not understand floated around her.

From a slight rise, the camp of the Israelites spread to the horizon, their numbers beyond imagining. In the distance, a great structure gleamed, caught by sunlight creeping over the edge of the world. To the east, the flurry of activity seemed different than the mourners standing in their tent openings. Rahab shaded her eyes. Were those wounded soldiers? Would they need help?

By the time she crossed to the tending of soldiers, bodies lay beneath the shade of a sycamore tree, covered with white linen death cloths. Rahab covered her mouth, but an injured youth stumbled to his knees. Rahab ran to his side. They allowed their youth to fight battles? What skill could this boy have against a seasoned warrior?

She pressed a rag to the wound on his forehead. He tried to speak, but she knew nothing of his language. She clicked her tongue instead, hoping to sooth him. Rough hands of a different man pushed her away from the boy. She landed in the dirt, her scarf falling back from her head.

"Why do that?" She glared but could not understand any sort of reply. The angry gesture waving her from the boy was obvious. "He's hurt. He needs attention." She stood. Jew or Canaanite, no man would treat her thus. Her hands pressed against her sides and she let her anger blaze.

He did not care for her response. His hand drew back intending to strike. Another man grabbed his arm. A stronger man.

"Salmon." Rahab looked down as she said his name. What right did she have to speak of him intimately? His family name was unknown to her.

Something was said. The other man gave her a hard look, then turned away. The injured youth groaned, and Rahab crouched beside him, wrapping a rag around the boy's wound.

"You know something of medicine?" Salmon handed her a long strip of fabric to use to secure the bandage.

"Why was he angry with me?"

Salmon shrugged. "You are a foreigner. A heavy hand has been dealt this day, by foreigners to the North. YHWH is displeased with us."

Rahab curled her nose in derision as she looked across the corpses. "You have sacrificed many to appease your god?"

"God does not require human sacrifice. These men

were killed in battle."

Fitting end for a warrior. "They should be honored, and their names immortalized."

Salmon shook his head. "That cannot be."

"Why not?"

"YHWH battles for us, at least He did in Jericho. Ai is a blip on the map compared to your great city, yet our men fled. There are dead and wounded."

"How can I help?"

"There is much chaos today. You hear the mourners. Joshua has rent his clothes and bows before the Lord for wisdom and knowledge. Return to your tents today. By tomorrow we will need help with supplies."

"Return here?"

Salmon shook his head. "The supply area is closer to you. Go there in the morning. You will find cloths for tearing strips."

His eyes gleamed with shadows. The events disturbed him. Rahab fisted her hand to repress the urge to touch his face, to offer comfort. "Send word if you have need."

"I will."

Seventh Day of the month of Iyar

"The heathens, they brought this about."

"YHWH warned us not to take anything from Jericho. He has repaid us with blood."

Rahab didn't need to understand the words crying from the gathering crowd. Eyes of men she'd never met blazed with hate. Women snarled. Rahab dropped the linen she'd been tearing for the wounded. Her throat closed as she sought a familiar face. Only strangers loomed, stepped closer.

Something struck her cheek. She gasped at the sting, reaching to cover the wound. Blood marred her hand when she pulled it away. "What are you doing?" She stumbled back, raising her arm against another projectile flung forward.

~

"Salmon!" Bezrah grabbed the pole of the tent to stop his momentum.

Salmon gazed at his friend while pressing a folded cloth on the soldier's wound. The gloom of Bezrah's look gave him pause. "What has happened?"

Bezrah nodded at the line of wounded men on the ground. "They're laying blame on Rahab."

"No." Salmon rushed to his feet, sweeping past Bezrah. "Where?" In the distance, Salmon noticed a haze of dust, raised voices carried on the wind. "YHWH protect her." He raced across the camp, thoughts of harm darkening his mood. Nothing could happen to her, his chest hurt at the idea of her in pain, or worse.

He heard her scream as he reached the edge of those who had gathered. "No." His voice boomed above the others. He pushed through, knocking a small stone from the hand of a cousin.

Rahab wavered as he broke through the line. He caught her up in his arms before she could fall. "What are you doing?" He screamed at the maddened crowd.

"She wasn't meant to be saved. How many of our own must die before the heathen and her family are put to death as they should have been?" The woman who cried wiped at her cheeks already smeared with dirt.

Salmon recognized her, a mother to a soldier who would not rise to fight again. "The defeat at Ai is not to her blame. Something else has caused this."

A man twice Salmon's age gripped a rock in his fist. "We were warned to take nothing. Our fathers perished in the desert. I'll not suffer the same fate."

"It is YHWH's hand that brought them from Jericho. She can help us learn cooking and how to turn grains to flour."

"She is a curse on us."

"Enough."

Joshua stepped beside Salmon. Even with clothes torn and ash smeared across his head, Joshua continued to command attention. He looked to the crowd, which silenced immediately. Then he faced Salmon. Salmon lowered his head but held on to the woman who shook in his arms.

Joshua lifted his hand. "Sanctify yourselves for tomorrow. The Lord God of Israel says there is an accursed thing among you. You cannot stand before your enemies until the accursed has been removed."

Mouths of a few opened, eyes accusing Rahab and Salmon. Joshua stopped them with a look. "In the morning, you will come by tribe. Whichever tribe the Lord marks, will come by family. Whichever family the Lord marks will come by household. Whichever household the Lord marks will come man by man." Joshua paused, and only the wind coursing across the valley could be heard. "The man that has transgressed against the Lord and against Israel will burn along with those closest and all their things." Joshua's voice deepened with anger. "They have transgressed the covenant of the Lord."

No one moved when Joshua finished. Salmon looked through the crowd. Evil brought evil. Thirty-six men dead, and more wounded.

Joshua waved them away. "Go."

Salmon set Rahab on her feet as the crowd dispersed. Blood marred her cheek and her eyes bounced from him to the angry people turning their backs.

"What has happened?" Rahab's voice skipped with a sob, but she stood her ground.

"Soldiers went against Ai thinking YHWH is with us. But they returned in defeat."

She nodded. "Why?"

"Someone has taken from Jericho and hidden it away."

Her eyes widened, cheeks paling. "Us."

"No." Salmon reassured. "Saving you and your family was sanctioned. This is another matter altogether." He looked across the camp encased by colors of twilight. "We are an impassioned people, given to run with our thoughts and ideas when we have cause to wait upon the Lord."

Rahab wrapped her arms around her chest. "Is this what will be? Something goes wrong and we are to blame?"

Salmon drew off his jacket and placed it around her. "I will find a way to protect you, by YHWH's grace. He has brought you this far."

She offered a hint of smile. "We are nowhere near the inn and what it offered."

Something in Salmon gripped his heart. "Would you rather be there?"

~

Waves of purple and pink crossed the sky above them as Rahab considered Salmon's question. Even through fear of the angry crowd, she hadn't thought coming from Jericho a mistake. She was scared, but YHWH... Strength washed through her. "This is where I want to be." She looked to Salmon. "I don't know how to get them to accept me."

"We will find a way." His smile brought an unusual warmth to her chest. He walked with her to the outskirts of camp. Tents for her parents and the twins remained intact. Malcontent had not boiled over to harm the others.

Salmon lifted his fingers toward her bleeding

cheek. "Allow me to get water to aid you."

"Mother will do it. What did your leader say to the people?"

"We are to cleanse ourselves and meet by tribe in the morning. Judgement will be made."

"How do you cleanse?"

"We wash. Husbands and wives will take separate sleeping quarters. Fresh clothes will be worn in the morning."

"Where do we go?"

"You remain here. Even should the mark be brought against the tribe of Judah, it will not be against our household."

"How can you know for certain?"

"Because YHWH is of truth. He cannot lie, by His very nature. This is not your fault."

Rahab gulped. Terror had been real, but she felt stronger now. "Thank you."

He did a strange thing. He kissed her forehead and walked away. Rahab stood watching him disappear into the darkness, holding his jacket around herself, and breathing his faint scent as she moved. What feelings were these?

~

Salmon rubbed his eyes as he returned to his tent. Kissing her was a mistake, especially as cleansing pertained to the mind as well as the body. But fear for her churned within. He cared more than was wise, unless something was to be done.

Eighth Day of the Month of Iyar

Morning light brought answers, and people remained close to their abode as Achan and his family were led away. None could lay blame at the Jerichobite and her family. Salmon closed his eyes and thanked YHWH yet again. The hours passed in solemn reflection. Those who returned from the valley of Achor were gray. The sun passed overhead, and then the trumpets blew, calling men to meet.

Salmon slipped beside Bezrah as they gathered. "Our next battle will prove successful."

Bezrah laughed. "Let us hope it involves less walking than Jericho."

Joking stopped as they beheld Joshua. All around, men stilled, leaned closer to the front. A sense of expectation energized the air.

"The accursed has been removed." Joshua had replaced his mourning garments with military attire. His voice carried across the crowd of men. "The Valley of Achor will not soon release its stench of burned flesh. The Lord God says we are ready to take Ai. YHWH permits you to take of your enemy. Spoils of cattle and possessions may return with you from the city once it has been rid of enemies. Report to your captains for direction in the upcoming battle." He raised his arms.

"Let us follow our forefathers' steps and reclaim our homeland."

Shouts echoed through camp. Salmon clamped Bezrah's shoulder. "Is your battle gear oiled? Guess we have a walk ahead of us after all."

"I will have your sister oil my gear." Bezrah jogged from Salmon's feigned punch, laughing.

Salmon grinned as they returned to their section of camp. The thought of Bezrah aligning with his sister did not disturb him. They would be brothers indeed. Another thought of marriage tickled his mind. Protection afforded by his name would cease all qualms against the strangers residing with them. The possibility brightened his smile.

Within a few hours, Salmon and Bezrah waited with the other soldiers of their legion. Captain Dayid stood tall at the front of their squadron holding his helmet beneath his arm. "Five legions will follow Caleb through the night. Our going must be silent. We will become the desert ghosts of which they murmur and fear. Wrap your weapons. We will follow the paths into the hills and set ourselves behind Ai in ambush. We must be in place before the sun rises." He began to pace. "Joshua will lead the bulk of our army into the valley tomorrow. The battle will take place early the following morning. When the men of Ai are drawn away, we will sweep into the city and set it to fire." He drew his sword, placed the tip against level ground, and marked the shadow. "Return within the hour with your supplies and food for the journey."

There was no need to carry his weapons with him to the tents, Salmon thought as he laid the narrow shield on the ground and placed his sword upon it. The shield had a wood base with a metal frame around it. Runes that symbolized the tribe of Judah had been carved into the wood. The shields he'd noticed of many of the Canaanites were wider but harder to wield. The width and length of Salmon's shield covered his chest and vital organs, and he could use it effectively as a tool not just defensively. He ran for the tents.

Ninth Day of the Month of Iyar

The gibbous moon had yet to set, but Salmon felt the midnight hour had passed. The walled city of Ai brandished torches in each of the towers, shining bright in their expected victory over Israel. He felt a burning in his chest as he followed the soldier in front of him. There would be no victory for Ai this time. Darkness surrounded them, but they were able to move bit by bit, following each other's footsteps as they passed the city below and turned into the mountain pass. Five thousand men trailed the line, yet Salmon could listen to the melody of locusts in the trees not far beyond their silent march.

The pale moon offered enough light to see yet not be seen. The oiled skin used to wrap his sword and shield was beginning to give off a rancid odor. His nose twitched. He would oil the cloths again before the next campaign. Perhaps Rahab could assist. Could she know an oil to use that would not spoil the way ram's fat did?

He pushed thoughts of Rahab from his mind. Now was not the time nor place. Not on the eve of battle. Ai faded from view as their legion was led into position. A signal passed through the lines after halting, and Salmon laid his weapons on the ground, taking a seat beside them. Their rustling sounded like wind moving through the rocky terrain. Dawn crept along the eastern horizon to his right. They had made it, as Captain Dayid planned. The day would be spent among the grasses that covered the pass. He laid across the ground as many other soldiers were doing. Using his helmet, he shielded his eyes from the brightening sky and let himself drift into a light sleep.

Rahab stood at the opening of her tent watching as morning's first light revealed a line of soldiers marching to the north. Was Salmon with them? Or had he been with the others who left in the night? What would it be like, marching into battle knowing your enemy would fall? The disgrace of three days ago had been cleansed. Today they moved forward with no fear of failure. Thoughts ran in her mind. Dog tilted its head to watch her. She picked up a stick. Its tail thumped. She tossed the stick and Dog chased after it. Moments later, the smaller dog joined the game.

Wind blew from the west with a cool touch and graced the day. Leti and Arron seemed to sense something different in the air. They plowed from their sleeping quarters long before their usual time. They climbed onto a fallen stump of tree to try to see the soldiers better. The dogs jumped up beside them.

"Where are they going? Will we be allowed to train as soldiers? How old do we have to be to train?" Their questions flew together, and Rahab could not tell which twin asked what. With a laugh, she grabbed them both and wrestled them down from their perch. They squealed, and then scrambled out of her grasp. Before long, the sound of sticks cracking against each other brought the twins' mother to the opening of her tent.

Malicha stilled them with a glance.

"Is that something you can teach me before I have children of my own?" Rahab asked as she joined her mother.

Malicha frowned. "To whom would you go to get with child? They have no temples in this place."

"I do not think temple mating is something practiced by this nation. I would join with one of their men to marry, if they will allow such a union." Salmon came to her mind, but for what purpose? He was a prince, far beyond her no matter the kindness that drew them together. The way his touch made her feel- no man had reached her heart save him.

"You do not mean to marry one of them?" Malicha gasped.

"If I am joined with a Jewish family, our family need not be considered strangers any longer. Leti and Arron will be able to go to school. We will learn their language."

"Why would they allow such freedoms? At best, we will be treated as servants."

Rahab shook her head. "I do not believe YHWH has saved us for such a role."

"Who is YHWH?"

"He is the God of Israel. I dreamt of Him." Rahab took her mother's hands. "A living God. He parted the river to allow His people to cross. He protected my home when the walls of Jericho fell. He is no statue, no sleeping giant refusing to be roused by the blood of children. He fights for them and gives them victory."

Malicha shook her head, eyes shadowed with doubt. "I do not understand these things."

Rahab grasped her mother's hands, squeezing them

with assurance. "You will learn. Give the God of Israel a chance."

As the sun peaked higher, Rahab stepped through the billowing curtains of her tent. Supplies for food dwindled. With a sack folded over her arm and basket upon her head, she crossed the southern edge of the camp until she reached the road leading toward the farms. Her feet slowed as she reached the farmer's market. No gray woman waited for a greeting. The makeshift shelter of three walls and thatched roof had been knocked over. The farmers would have sought shelter at Jericho. Rahab looked in the direction of the fallen city. Her throat tightened. Only five members of her family remained because the God of Israel drew her. "What am I to such a one as He?" she whispered as she searched the fields bending with harvest.

Israelite women stood among the wavering grains. Rahab frowned. They seemed to be trying to cut the tips of the plants rather than the stalks. If they didn't clear the stalks, the fields wouldn't be good for planting in the next season. She crossed to the nearest group, offering a hesitant smile. The front woman, dark hair tied back in a braid, neither frowned nor smiled.

"May I?" Rahab reached out for the cutting knife being used on the wheat, heart thumping with hope of not being injured.

The woman sighed, took the knife by its flat side, and offered the handle toward Rahab.

Rahab grabbed a handful of wheat stalks a few spaces from the ground, swung the knife, and showed the woman she had cut most of the plant from the earth. "I can show you how to use the shafting bowls as well." Rahab tossed the bundle in her basket.

But the woman turned away. Rahab blinked, why couldn't they see her as anything but an enemy? Bitterness made her grimace. She grabbed another handful of wheat and struck with the blade. She tossed the bundle in the basket. *Let them fumble, if they are too proud to accept my help. What do desert wanderers know of crops? Their breads will be hard and heavy, barely palpable.*

She kept her head down and worked. If she didn't see them, maybe she would forget they were near, and the tight grip of her chest would loosen. Except they came closer to where Rahab worked and their strange language louder. When Rahab looked, a small group of women stood little more than an arm's length from her, one of them the woman who lent her the knife. "What do you want?" Did they mean to strike her down? Spill her blood in the field? She stood taller, but the gathered group held no malice toward her. She could not understand the language babbling from them, but they gestured at the gathered wheat in her basket and the bundle she still held in her hand.

"This?"

The first woman made a chopping motion. They wanted to see what she had shown? Something in her heart lightened as she grabbed another handful of wheat and slashed the blade close to the earth. They pointed at her filling basket.

"Do you know how to use the shafter?" Of course, they couldn't understand her. She lifted the basket and motioned for them to follow. She led them to one of the jumbled lean-tos. She pushed patches of thatch to the side, digging beneath in hopes of finding the bowl and pestle she sought. They kept their distance from the ruin. *Not helpful,* Rahab thought as she tugged a wood board out of the way. She found a bowl of cracked plain pottery, with the tools nestled inside of it. They still refused to come closer. She lifted the bowl, barely managing to wrap her arms around the circumference, and staggered closer to them. When she dropped her burden on the ground beside the gathered group, she went back to retrieve her basket and sack.

Upon returning, she sat, wedging the bowl with her feet. The pestle was heavy, about the size of her forearm. She held it in a fist, placed a handful of wheat heads inside the bowl, then rubbed the pestle over them with swift, circular movements. She turned the stalks, continuing to use the pestle to rub wheat grains from the plants.

The first woman took hold of the pestle when Rahab set it aside to gather a second handful of wheat. The women studied the thick rounded head, rubbing it against the palms of their hands. They looked at the seeds in the bowl.

Rahab lifted the bowl, tilting it slightly, and blowing across the top. Shafts drifted into the air, away from the seed. The women leaned closer and gathered seed remaining in the bowl, letting it drift through their fingers, chattering. Rahab held the bowl to the first woman. "You, try?"

She used a different word, tapping her chest.

Rahab shrugged and nodded, uncertain what had been said. The woman sat, so Rahab assumed she meant to try. The Israelite woman obviously wasn't used to pinning pottery with her feet. Rahab crouched beside her, helping her learn to wedge the bowl. She then turned her hand on the pestle.

"That's right," Rahab nodded as the woman rolled the pestle across a handful of wheat. The woman smiled, brightening her face. The others seemed just as pleased.

"Anasha." The woman tapped herself.

"Anasha? You?" Rahab tried to repeat the word. A name?

"Anasha."

Rahab pointed to herself. "Rahab."

"Rahabeia." They struggled with the hard sound in her name, but Rahab didn't care. They wanted to make themselves known to her, and that mattered more than anything. She wanted to giggle, she wanted to dance. She wanted to share the moment with Salmon.

Her cheeks heated, but no one seemed to notice. They glanced at the ruin nearby and at the bowl. They would need more. Farmers usually kept half a dozen sets at the posts for reapers to use. She set to looking for more, leaving the others to work on their harvest.

Rahab managed to find three additional bowls, along with an extra pestle. She learned a few more names. Helbereth. Marita. Chernith. Rahab tried repeating each name, wondering at the mix of sounds she had never noticed before. "Th." She tried to repeat the segment but couldn't without spitting. They laughed. Not a harsh sound, but one of companionship.

They needed to let the grains dry. Rahab wasn't sure she got the idea through to them, but she didn't mind the walk back to the tents for her family. The sack-covered basket weighed little as she carried it on her head. She would go on the morrow for more. Perhaps they would listen, and she could teach them how to grind the grains into flour.

On the pass above Ai, the soldiers spent their day hiding in the grasses, doing their best to ignore the buzz of insects embracing the spring day. The sound of drums muttered in the air, letting them know the main army moved into position across the valley. When the sun was a hands-width from twilight, a signal passed through the legions. Salmon crept to the council quarter with the other leaders of the legions. He crouched as Captain Zechariah used a stick to draw the outer wall of the city of Ai in the dirt.

"Joshua will send the bulk of soldiers into the valley before the dawn. They will draw soldiers of Ai from the city. The battle will go poorly." Captain Zechariah raised his eyebrows.

Salmon caught his meaning and smirked as he realized what would happen.

Captain Zechariah continued. "Joshua and his men will have to turn and flee as happened before. When the soldiers of the city are drawn far enough away, we will set an ambush against all those who remain within the walls." He gave a look around those gathered. "None are to be kept alive. You may take spoils and cattle as you find, after the city has been taken and burned."

Clever plan. Salmon relayed the words of the captain to those in his charge. Cold victuals provided sustenance and they waited for the greater part of Joshua's army to make their move.

Tenth Day of the Month of Iyar

Soldiers hiding in the mountain pass above Ai alerted as the sound of battle gear clanked in the predawn. The darkness of land and tree against the sky hinted at the nearness of morning, but Salmon quietly gathered his gear and prepared with the others. The warriors of Ai thought they could reach out and defeat the Israeli army at their doorstep? Salmon shook his head. Why had they not given heed to the warning sent before the Israelite campaign to retake their homeland reached their borders?

Salmon crouched with the other soldiers, watching and listening. His leather boots protected his feet and calves from the tickling touch of grasses beginning to grow beneath the warmth of the spring sun. the vesture tunic had strips of hardened leather sewn into fabric, overlapping as it reached his chest and shoulders. Rather than keeping his arms bare as some soldiers preferred, Salmon had leather wraps around his forearms as well. He unwrapped his sword, watching the glint of starlight on the metal, before wrapping the oiled skins and his small pack of provisions together. He left them sitting against a tree.

The stars dimmed and the gray curtain of night lifted to pale yellow and blue sky. The soldiers of Ai were running from the gates of the city into the valley as the colors of dawn faded. Scouters of the Israelite army watched for the signal from Joshua. Excitement flowed through the ranks as the line of enemies marched further from the city.

When the signal came, Joshua raising his standard high, the five legions waiting in the mountain pass beyond the city moved forward. Salmon stepped over a rock and continued down the path. He brandished his sword, the swirling movement in line with the rush of adrenaline coursing into his blood. Thought faded as he crossed the outer wall of the city. A frenzy of screams tore into the morning. The battle began.

Blood dripped from his sword. Enemies lay slaughtered across the dirt floor. It didn't matter they were women and children. Evil held the hearts of the older. YHWY would make better use of the young in paradise. Salmon kicked aside an overturned trunk. Fabrics dyed in colors of purple and blue spilled onto the floor. He nabbed them before they touched puddles of blood. He tucked them away, spoils he would take with him. He stepped from the hut, crouched at a patch of dirt and grass to clean his sword. The cry of soldiers returning to the city sounded. Eagerness moved him. He brandished his sword, swinging it in an arc as he ran for the gates.

Before long, fire raged through the city. Israelite troops moved along the streets, gathering those things they desired. Jewels could be melted and refined. Skins of fur and leather could be useful when winter came. Salmon laid claim to a wagon and a pair of oxen to pull it. He and Bezrah piled their goods in the base of the wagon. Rahab and her family would find the cart and animals useful.

"My satchel and skins remain in the pass. Let us go retrieve those things." Salmon unhooked his tunic and laid it over the side of the wagon. Sweat stained the undergarment, but the touch of air on his skin felt good.

"At the least you could have left your supplies against the outer wall." Bezrah teased. "You want to walk the mountain after battle?"

A grove of olive trees had been planted across the lower hills. Rather than walk the long way around to the path leading up the mountain pass, Salmon and Bezrah cut through the trees. Dappled light cast shadows across the mottled-colored ground. Branches groaned as a wind blew through the grove. Salmon laughed, slapping his hand on Bezrah's shoulder. Bezrah stopped without warning, holding his hand in a signal of silence. Something moved ahead of them. A man slipped through the trees, but he did not wear the garb of an Israelite soldier.

Salmon raised two fingers and motioned to his right. He pointed at Bezrah and motioned left. Bezrah pulled a dagger from his belt. Salmon shrugged. His sword remained with his protective tunic. He crouched and selected a thick branch almost as long as Bezrah's dagger. With a nod, the two men separated and set to track the stranger through the grove.

He would have preferred something a bit more like a forged sword, but Salmon appreciated the feel of strength in the branch he held. He watched the stranger sprint to a tree, give a quick look around it, and then run to the next. Salmon slipped out of view every time the other man's head turned in his direction. He drew closer. This was no ordinary stranger. The medallion dangling from a chain about his neck held a royal insignia.

Bezrah was getting close as well. Salmon motioned, wrapping his left hand around his right fist. They needed to take down the stranger but not kill. This one would need to go to Joshua. Bezrah's nod indicated he understood.

Salmon hid the branch behind his back and stepped out where he might be seen. "Murderers! All of them murderers." He cried out in the Canaanite language. The stranger swirled around drawing a blade. Salmon raised his left hand, trying to indicate he held no weapon. "Do you run for Bethel? Our neighbors will protect us, can they not? They will avenge the dead?"

"You are no son of Ai." The stranger scowled, lines of hate and fear crossing his face as he took a step closer.

"Neither is he," Salmon replied in Hebrew and swung his branch through the air.

Bezrah cried out and knocked into the stranger. Though the larger man staggered, he did not fall. The clank of sword against sword rang through the grove. Salmon ducked and knocked the stranger's feet out from under him. The man fell hard, his sword falling from his grasp. Bezrah pressed the heel of his boot on the beefy hand. "I think Joshua will be interested in meeting you."

The man continued to struggle but could not free himself. Bezrah unhooked his belt. They forced the stranger onto his back and pulled his hands together, looping the belt tight around his wrists. With a grunt, Salmon and Bezrah pulled him to his feet and forced him to walk between them.

"Grab his sword." Bezrah nodded at the jewel-crusted hilt. Salmon pulled the scabbard from the stranger and tied it around his own waist, putting the weapon away where it could not be retrieved easily by their prisoner. They headed for the burning city of Ai.

Not much time passed before they noticed Joshua leading a band of soldiers around the wall of the city.

"Sir," Salmon bowed. "We found him slinking through the trees towards Bethel."

Bezrah tossed Joshua the chain and medallion that had hung against the stranger's chest. "He still wore this."

Joshua caught the medallion with one hand. He glanced at the inscribed circle of gold and then pulled the woven cap from the prisoner's head. The man growled and fought against them, but Bezrah nabbed a handful of hair and pulled his head back.

Joshua sneered. "You wear commoner clothes, but your image is posted throughout the city. You would run in battle? Have you no duty to your soldiers and your people? What manner of king are you?"

Salmon repeated the words in the common Canaanite tongue. The king spat.

"You were loath to give up your crest. Now we shall hang you with it." He looked at Salmon, and then at an ancient olive tree with branches bending close to the earth. "Drag him over there."

Joshua used a dagger to cut the cord of the medallion. He knotted the ends into a hangman's loop and tied it with a longer rope. The king of Ai screamed, writhing against them. Bezrah knocked the hilt of his sword across the king's forehead. In the brief stillness, they managed to slip the noose over his head and tighten the knots. Salmon ignored the vile curses that flew from the man's lips as they hoisted him onto a donkey. Several other soldiers joined them, lending aid to pull the noose over a tree branch, testing the branch for soundness.

The crazed bucking of the king frightened the donkey and it scrambled from beneath him. The soldiers had barely managed to secure the rope when the full weight of the king pulled it taut. Spittle dripped from the king's tongue which hung from his open mouth as his feet jerked. The violence of his body's convulsions cracked his neck, and the feet stilled. His eyes bulged, blood coating the left eye. The creak of the rope rocking back and forth was the only sound to be heard. The acrid smell of urine rose as liquid poured down the king's leg and dripped into the dirt.

Joshua brushed his hands off. "Let him hang until the last light of the day."

Salmon held the sword belonging to the king toward Joshua. "This was his."

"Is it a decent weapon?" Joshua asked as they moved away from the olive tree.

Salmon swung the sword in an arc. The thin blade whistled as air moved across it. "I believe the weapon is well forged."

"You may keep it if you like. The sword may prove useful against our enemies."

Salmon returned it to the scabbard wrapped around his waist. He grinned at Bezrah. "We still need to gather my things."

The smoke that wafted from the burning city held the scent of burning flesh. Most of the soldiers who did not continue to sift through the goods of Ai moved southwest in order to hold the breeze to their backs rather than face into it. Joshua called Salmon and two other captains to him.

"Cut down the king, throw his body in the gate of the wall and have your men pile stones upon him. You will sleep tonight here in the valley with the rest of us, but on the morrow, your troops will return to the camp at Gilgal. I and the others travel into the mountains. YHWH has shown me a location up the valley where we can build an alter and offer sacrifice for the battle won."

"Will you stay long?" Captain Dayid asked.

Joshua shook his head. "My heart burns within me. It is long since we heard and listened to the words of YHWH told us through Moses. Gather the people. The camp remains in Gilgal, bring only what they will need for a day's journey and return. After the sacrifices, I will speak the covenant, the blessings, and the curses wrought between YHWH and His people."

Salmon rubbed his hands together, crossing the flat land of the valley as he searched for the pendant that marked his legion. Everyone was bid come to listen to the reading by Joshua, even the strangers among them. The familiar design of the flag flapped in the breeze sweeping up to the mountains. He turned to the right. Shading his eyes with his hand, he was able to find the wagon and beasts. He dropped his satchel in the bed of the wagon then motioned for the team leaders to join him. News travelled swiftly. Battle wearied soldiers laid against their supplies and dozed. Salmon would have liked a bit of respite himself, but the sun was setting, and they had a body to cut down from the olive tree. He settled for a gulp of water, splashing a few drops on his face. He turned back toward the city.

Bezrah joined the small group as they stood at the olive tree. Though the sun had dipped below the horizon, light still showed the blank gaze of death. Blue veins crossed skin turned pasty-white. Someone cut the rope and the carcass dropped to the ground with a thud. Captain Dayid kicked the body over and another soldier cut the binding to his hands. It took four of them to lift the dead king, two at his feet and two at his shoulders. The order to find stones had been given. The body was tossed in the way of the gate, and rocks of various sizes piled on top of him. The heap reached from one side of the gate to the other, cascading over like a mountain in miniature. The main entrance into the city of Ai was blocked.

Eleventh Day of the Month of Iyar

Morning came swiftly. A small contingency
of soldiers turned southeast towards Gilgal as the main
host started the march up the valley. Birds squawked,
their ardent voices reverberating through the decimated
city of Ai. *A feast indeed*, Salmon thought.

The journey back to camp did not require the
stealth silence of their attack on the city. Soldiers joked,
jostling each other. Salmon and Bezrah had not
acquired the only cart and cattle, and the sound of
braying along with the stench of battle-weary soldiers
and field beasts mingled. Salmon glanced at the fabrics
stored in the wagon. Bilhah and Elia may like the
brighter colors. As might Rahab. The tools for working
the earth rattled as the wheels rumbled across uneven
ground. *Was it possible they could have a life within
their own city? Have a house with land for a kitchen
garden?* Almost it seemed more than he could imagine.

"You remain quiet this morning. Are your thoughts
troubled?" Bezrah joined him.

"No such thing. Wondering what life might be
when we have redeemed our homeland."

Bezrah laughed. "Can you imagine? Caleb speaks
of the mountain he desires, but what of the rest of us?"

"YHWH must have a plan. Have you talked with

Meishal about marrying my sister?"

Bezrah's cheeks reddened and Salmon had to keep from laughing at his best friend. "How could you think that?" Bezrah stuttered.

"The two of you work well together. The idea makes sense."

"What of you? Is there a woman with whom you would mate?"

It was Salmon's turn to look at the ground kicked up by thousands of feet marching to and from the city.

Bezrah still knew where his thoughts had taken him. "You would take the stranger that has come to us?"

"She is brave. Beautiful. The hand of YHWH is upon her."

"But you are a prince of Judah, will your family allow such an alliance?"

"My station may be what makes this work. Her family needs protection. I can offer them that."

Bezrah whistled. "I do not envy your taking this to the priests, or your uncle—or her family for that matter. There are many who will need convincing."

Excitement across the camp was palpable. Soldiers had returned. Not all of them, but there was no sense of distraught to suggest disaster had befallen them. Exuberance made her smile, though she understood little of what was being said as she moved closer.

"Rahab."

The sound of Salmon's voice made her heart leap. She closed her eyes. She didn't want the slew of emotion regarding him. His friendship, yes, but there could be nothing more between them. She opened her eyes and turned to face him. He tugged on the yoke of a pair of oxen. A wagon rolled behind the beasts. "What have you brought?" The animals smelled almost as bad as the camp refuse which seemed to move closer to where Rahab's family's tents had been set. The dogs scattered.

The pleasure of seeing him outweighed any hesitation. He was fresh from war, though some effort had been made to clear his uniform.

"A gift for you." His eyes glittered with delight. "But first I bid you and your family come. The boys and your parents may ride in the wagon. We have a long way to journey. Joshua has a special reading he is preparing."

"A reading of what?" She frowned. "We will not understand him."

"I will interpret for you. He shares the words of Moses, our most beloved leader. Moses led us out of Egypt. He guided us through the wilderness." Salmon stepped closer to her. "My father was captain of Judah's fighting men. When I was young, he told me Moses spoke with YHWH. Moses stood with Him. They covered Moses with a veil because the light of the Holy One was too great for any to look upon him without trembling in fear. My father died in the wilderness, but Moses led us to the edge of the promised land."

"Will his words teach us of YHWH?"

"Yes, the words written by Moses teach us of YHWH. There is much you will be able to learn. Bring food and drink and let us go with the gathering."

Rahab walked beside Salmon for a while, but the glances of his people brought heat to her cheeks and she finally excused herself to speak with her family. She did not know what to expect from the half-day journey. The wide, flat valley dotted with shrubs and weeds narrowed as the caravan drew closer to two rolling hills leading up into the mountains, one to the south and one to the north. Mount Ebal and Mount Gerizim, Rahab recognized them from illustrations and descriptions of travelers who had stayed at the inn. The mass of people across the valley were unrecognizable. On the mountain to the north, against the backdrop of deep blue sky, a massive structure had been built.

"What is that?" Rahab asked Salmon who remained near their little group.

He looked in the direction she pointed. "The alter to YHWH. If you were to draw near, you would see the alter has been built with twelve stones, one for each of the tribes of Israel."

"Twelve stones? How could it be so large with only twelve?"

"The stones may not be cut. Many men are needed to move and arrange the stones." He smiled. "It will not easily be broken down either. We will be able to come for years to see it."

Something glinted from the other mountain. "What is that?" Rahab could not identify detail, and yet something upon Gerizim shone.

Salmon bowed his head. "The Levites, our priests, carry the Ark of the Covenant with them. You may have seen them carrying the Ark as we marched around Jericho. It is a sacred relic to our people. YHWH himself sits upon the seat between the angels."

Rahab wrapped her arms around herself. "He is here now? Is that what shines?"

Salmon grinned, one side of his mouth lifting. "No. The ark has been covered with gold. The sun is what makes it shine. A great cloud will settle upon the tabernacle and you will know God is with us."

A visual sign? Not even the magicians of Jericho could produce a vision of cloud. Rahab remained silent. Salmon leaned against the wagon. "Joshua has sacrificed rams in honor of victory." Salmon explained further. The twins hung on the front of the wagon, stretching up on their knees to see what was going on. Her parents welcomed Salmon with a wary glance.

"I will share with you as Joshua begins to read." He placed his hand on her arm. "If you are willing to hear." He looked to her parents. "All of you."

His hand dropped away, yet Rahab could feel the warmth of his touch remain. "I will listen." *I will listen to stand near him, to hear his voice, and to understand more of YHWH, the God who has brought me from death.* Her thoughts could not deny the desire of her heart.

"We would like to listen as well." Her parents nodded.

Joy filled Salmon. The words spoken by Joshua held Moses in them. He could hear Moses' voice speaking the words. Joshua spoke, and Salmon repeated the laws, blessings, and curses in the Canaanite language. Rahab's parents forgot their fear and attended to what was said, leaning closer as their eyes filled with wonder. The twins scooted nearer. Rahab wiped tears from her cheeks as she heard the blessings to come from God.

Hours passed quickly, and Joshua prayed over

them all. The small group sat together, no other of Salmon's tribe joining them, in the late afternoon eating bread. No one seemed capable of breaking the silence, and yet it was a peaceful, reflective silence. Memories of Moses passed through his mind. What would he have thought of the beautiful dark-haired Rahab? Strangers enjoyed sanctuary among them. It hurt to see Rahab discomfited. He looked at Leti and Arron. The boys needed lessons in language and becoming soldiers. Salmon finished his serving of bread and stood. "We will return to Gilgal. The trail will be easy to follow even when night falls."

"Thank you for your generosity toward us," Malicha reddened and looked down as she spoke to him. "I am in all astonishment at your God."

"He is your God now, too. The true living God."

"We thank you." Rahab whispered, her dark eyes swimming with unshed tears.

Gratitude, he could read the emotion on her face. Any doubt in his heart melted away. He determined the path he would take.

Twelfth Day of the Month of Iyar

"A fine day, son. A very fine day." Meishal hugged Salmon.

Salmon laughed at the wide grin on his uncle's face. "What has brought this delight?"

"An offer of marriage has come for your sister. A good match, I think she and you will agree."

"Bezrah?" Joy leapt in his breast at Meishal's nod. "He asked? I was not certain he would find the courage."

Meishal laughed. "He was a bit pale and sweaty-more so than usual. He seemed pleased by my agreement."

"I am happy for them. She will not find a better husband. He has been a true friend all my life. Now he will be my brother."

"I have looked upon you as my own son since your father died. It would please me even more to know you have a family of your own. With your friend settled, will you be willing to accept a wife?"

Salmon took a deep breath. The time had come. "I have a thought, but I am uncertain how well it will be accepted."

Meishal shook his head, features darkening. "I know of what you speak. Your interest in the outskirts of Gilgal have been noticed. She is a foreigner."

"She need not remain so."

"Upon this I cannot give my blessing." He raised a hand as Salmon prepared to protest. "You must take your address to the elders. It is their decision if they will permit such a union."

Salmon stepped closer to his uncle. "If they grant my request? Will you bestow your blessing then?"

Meishal rubbed his hand across his eyes. "I would have you unite with a Jewish woman. I do not understand why you would do otherwise. But neither do I understand YHWY's purpose in preserving the family of a nation we set to destroy." He sighed. "If permission is granted, I will not stand in your way." He gave him a hard look. "Your mother may require stronger persuasion."

Salmon grasped Meishal by the shoulders. "Thank you, Uncle."

He knew to whom he needed to speak. Crossing the camp to the tent of Oshnish, an elder Levi priest, did not take long. Salmon nabbed a stalk of hay as nerves made his heart race. Of all the tribes of Israel, only the tribe of Levi did not fall under the curse given at the cowardice of the original spies into the promised land. Caleb and Joshua remained much unchanged throughout Salmon's life, but Oshnish had grown a hoary head with reddish liver spots marring the skin on his face and arms. It was to him he went for spiritual matters. To Oshnish, Salmon would appeal permission to marry Rahab.

Salmon chewed the end of a hay stalk. "I will take her to wife."

"Don't be a fool." His brother, Sepher, pushed into

the tent.

Salmon spun from Oshnish. "What are you doing here?"

"Uncle confided your purpose. This is not a good idea."

"Remaining outside the camp is not safe. Did we spare Rahab and her family at Jericho to allow death from another source?"

"Perhaps this is as it should be."

Salmon gripped his hands into fists. "God spared her family. He spared Rahab. We have only to look upon the wall to see where His hand prevented the fall of her house. This is by God's design."

"Salmon speaks truth." Oshnish waved at the brothers.

Sepher frowned. "Then let her marry a lesser son of a lesser family." His attention returned to Salmon. "You are prince of the House of Judah. Your destiny lies elsewhere."

Salmon shook his head, allowing the weed to drift from his fingers and fall to the earth. "I am determined. My path will join with Rahab. Her family will be my family. By my name, they will be free to move within our camps."

"She lived on the wall." Sepher stepped closer, lowering his voice. "Her business involved relations with travelers."

"Matters not, brother. She has embraced the God of Abraham, Isaac, and Jacob."

"You've met with her?" His lips curled with derision. "Since the battle?"

"Our paths have crossed. She prepared straps for the wounded. Her brothers learn to tend horses." He stood taller. "I translated the words of Moses for them at Mount Ebal."

Sepher shook his head and stepped back. "You admire the woman? The harlot?"

"She risked her life to save ours."

"To betray her own people."

"She's dreamt of the Lord. He gave her faith in the one true God. From that moment to this, her family have no people. Under my protection, they will be one of us. Marrying her is the right thing to do."

"Have you had many conversations with her?"

The elder stood. "Enough." His voice captured the brothers' attention. Salmon faced the aged man of YHWH who had taught him much. "Salmon, if you mean to do this, there is no turning back. She will not be put away. Is there none of your tribe you would rather marry?"

"There is no one. My mind has set on Rahab."

"What of your heart?"

"By YHWH's grace, my heart turns toward her as well. I will have her."

Sepher growled. "You've fallen in love with the harlot? Mother will not stand for this."

"Mother will accept my decision. She will be eager for lives to come."

Once again, Oshnish interrupted their heated discussion by raising his hand between their faces. "In this you will allow Rahab to choose. Will you accept her to wife if her choice is never to warm your bed?"

The steadiness of his heart did not falter as he faced his mentor. "I will protect her to the end of my days, regardless of the manner of our relationship." He nodded. "I will respect her decision."

Sepher backed away. "I have voiced my concern. If you mean to do this, so be it. Do not expect everyone to accept your decision with blessing."

Salmon knelt before Oshnish. "Elder, I would have your blessing."

The old man placed his hand upon Salmon's head. "Stranger things than I understand have worked here. May the blessing of God be with you, son."

The refuse of the camps seemed to be moving closer to Rahab and her family. A finger against his nose did not stop the stench wafting on a breeze. Rahab sat in the doorway of a tent, leaning over a bowl as she razed kernels of maize from long husks. She wore her dark hair braided to her back. The exotic clothes he'd seen her wear in Jericho had been replaced with traditional Jewish dress.

A pair of excited screams nabbed his attention. Small bodies of Leti and Arron swept against him, nearly knocking him from his feet.

"Salmon, Salmon." Their hands grabbed at him, laughing as they turned him about.

"Did you bring us horse lessons?"

"I've grown an inch, at least. I should be ready to ride."

He lunged an arm around each of them and dragged them from their feet. Screams of delight erupted as they wiggled against him. He looked up as Rahab stood, her laughter setting an odd beat to his heart. He grinned at her. "I seem to have caught a pair of fish. Odd, they should be swimming in air as they do."

"They certainly stink like fish." She swatted at her

brothers. "Let them go. They have chores to complete."

"But the horse…"

"—he needs us."

Salmon ruffled their curly hair. "Horse will be here when you finish. Obedience is important."

The boys ran away. Rahab's almond shaped eyes laughed at him. "The work will not be done well."

"They are good lads."

"They are. As long as we are careful. I would not see them hurt."

"The edge of camp is not a safe dwelling place, I know."

"We have no other choice. There is no where we can go where we will be safe."

"Come further in."

Her laugh did not contain humor. "Your people will not allow us to move among you."

"Our people."

She sneered. "I remain an Amorite. They will not let us forget."

"Do you worship those gods? Could you join another city among the Canaanites?"

"You know we have nothing."

"Would you go back and choose a different path?"

She drew her coat around her, facing the sun heading toward the west before looking at him. "Not having met your God."

"Our God. You claim him, do you not?"

"I am a dog. What would your God have to do with me?"

"He saved you."

"You saved us. Our agreement. Your lives for ours."

"I had nothing to do with your part of the wall remaining intact as the rest crumbled to dust. That power is God's alone."

"Why would He save us and none other?"

"Because your heart turned to Him. God chose Israel, yes, to be his peculiar people, but salvation is intended for all." He breathed. "Join with me. Allow me to offer you the protection of my name."

Her cheeks deepened to a rosy hue. "I cannot. That life no longer appeals to me."

"I offer marriage by whatever terms you decide."

"Marriage?" Her gaze searched him. He could read her confusion and something else—perhaps hope? "Us? But why?" Her voice softened.

He took a step closer. Her eyes widened, but she didn't back up. Salmon took it as a good sign. "Can you not guess? Your faith lays mine to shame. You, having been raised on false gods, aligning yourself to the Living God? Stepping out in faith and courage? How could I not love you?"

Her arms wrapped protectively around her front. "I have known men much of my life, but I have not known love."

Salmon reached his hand to brush against her cheek. "Then allow me to teach you. Do you understand what marriage means?"

"Yes." Her gaze slid to the dirt. "We will be together."

"Our parents will work a contract. In it, all of you will have a safe haven. After the contract is signed, our two lives become one." He touched her chin and with a gentle push, lifting her face to see him. "Your family will move to the tents of my family."

"I do not want babies. I will not risk them to sacrifice."

"We have atoning sacrifice, yes, but they are of animal flesh and blood. No Jewish child will lay upon the alters of a hungry god. No foreign child among us will either."

"How can that be?"

"There is time to learn, and much to be learned. Say yes."

She sighed. "It is best for all of us."

How could he desire to join his family to hers? Rahab knew it would benefit her family, but what of his? A measure of joy dimmed in his eyes, and her throat tightened.

"Blessings will fall upon us." He promised.

He made to turn away, and she nabbed his arm. "Salmon?"

He stopped. "Yes, my dear."

His direct gaze made her feel as though she were a precious jewel. Her insides buzzed with life. "My heart is for you. I do not understand why, there can be nothing for you in joining with me. You would be better served with a wife of your tribe."

"YHWH has brought me on a path that leads to you. If you do not wish to live as husband and wife, I can respect your choice. My name will protect you all."

Her hand remained on his arm, the warmth of him seeping through her. Did she desire to lay with him? More than any man she'd met. She frowned. "I want more than just your name."

He smiled knowingly. "Because you love me too."

He kissed her, and thoughts of any other man faded

away. She was home.

Thirteenth Day of the Month of Iyar

Arron and Leti's shouts of delight along with dogs barking drew Rahab's attention. She walked from the tent, brushing her hands on her apron. Sight of Salmon made her heart race. He hadn't come alone. A young woman, looking uncomfortable, rode a horse beside him. Tendrils of black hair loosed from her braid. She seemed young, younger than Salmon at least. She peered at Rahab then lowered her face. Salmon slid from his horse first, and then helped the unknown woman.

"The boys will care for the horses. They have been quick learners."

Rahab didn't understand what Salmon said to the woman. Neither could her brothers, but they eagerly accepted responsibility for the animals sent their direction. Salmon and the woman walked toward Rahab. The stranger offered a hesitant lift of her lips then looked at Salmon. His smile eased the tension.

"This is my sister, Elia." He placed a hand on her shoulder. "She would like to learn how you are able to make the bread that has a sweet taste."

"You don't know how to bake bread?" Rahab twisted her hands in her apron.

"Our lives in the desert afforded little opportunity

to cook. The women from the field speak of all you showed them."

"How could you survive without preparing food?"

"YHWH provided our food both morning and night, on all days save the Sabbath."

Questions swirled in her mind. How could a god provide food every day for years? What, did it fall from the sky? She opened her mouth to ask, but a glance at Elia showed the young woman's anxiety. The girl's eyes darted as though she were frightened. Rahab softened her smile. "I would be pleased to teach you, Elia." She repeated the name slowly, trying to pronounce it like Salmon had. The girl's smile widened.

"Ra Hab." Elia tried pronouncing Rahab's name.

Rahab held her hand to her. "Come."

Salmon nodded, and Elia took Rahab's hand. Rahab led her to the prep area. Instead of shelves locked onto a wall for storage, they had crates that could be stacked. Rahab placed the items they would need on the table.

She dipped her hand into the first pouch and showed Elia. "We call this flour. It is made from the grains growing in the field.

"Flour." Elia repeated.

Salmon touched what was in her hand. "We used it to make unleavened bread."

Rahab went through the other ingredients, letting them taste the grapes. She laughed at Elia's puckered face.

As they waited for the bread to rise, Rahab lit a fire in the stone oven outside the tent. She offered them tea as they waited, the three of them sat together. Elia taught Rahab the months of the year and days of the week. They all laughed at her pronunciations. Leti and Arron joined them, leaning against Rahab.

"Will we have to learn more of this language?" Leti wrapped his arms around Rahab's neck.

"You won't have much difficulty, seeing how you like to talk." Rahab laughed at him.

"I am as smart as Leti. I will learn as fast." To prove it, Arron went through the list of months and days. Salmon and Elia clapped when he finished.

"You have a sweet sister," Rahab's smile held a hint of sadness.

Salmon touched her cheek before his thoughts could prevent him. "I am sorry for your loss."

"They made the wrong choice, not for lack of my trying."

"I praise YHWH you are with us." The color in his cheeks heightened. "That your family will join with mine."

His glance caused fluttering in her stomach. Elia grinned. Rahab looked away from Salmon. "Will you come back for more cooking lessons?"

Salmon interpreted for them. Elia's smile grew as she nodded.

Rahab felt joy in her chest. "Mother and I have much we can teach." She hugged Leti and Arron. "You can teach us more of your language."

Arron tugged on Rahab's ponytail. "Is the bread ready for eating?"

She pushed him away, then went to the oven. Using two sticks, she pulled the tanned dough. Elia joined her, holding a platter. Rahab pulled the bread onto the platter. The twins bounced around them, but the women held the platter aloft.

"It is too hot," Rahab chided. "A little patience will be worth not burning your mouth."

Elia said something. Rahab looked at Salmon.

"They are like any other boys of Judah." He laughed.

Rahab allowed Elia to take the platter into the tent. She remained close to Salmon. "They will find welcome with your people?"

"As will you all. Are you ready to begin marriage preparations?"

This precious man would be hers, and she would be his. She nodded. "I am ready."

Even though he did not touch her, she read excitement in his gaze. They walked, side by side, to the tent to break bread together.

Many days later-

Marriage to Salmon brought strange custom. Salmon and Meishal brought a contract to Dassub. The family was granted space among the sons of Judah. With the contract signed, a merry party of women dressed in white danced around Rahab as they brought her to Salmon's tent. Rahab lay with her husband, within his tent while a party raged outside. There was no virginity cloth to produce, and yet Salmon offered something no other man ever had. He offered love. He offered her a child.

Rahab rubbed the side of her stomach. A tiny foot pushed against her hand even as another spasm gripped her in pain. She cried out, the other women in the birthing tent raising their voices with her. The pain passed, and she fell back against the cushions of her bed. Malicha pressed a cool cloth across her forehead. Words drifted around her, but she closed her eyes and focused on the body writhing within her. The little one was determined to gain access to the world soon.

More pain tore at her, but then Rahab heard the soft cry of new life. Sobs of joy wracked her chest, mingling with the hurt that lingered at the infant's birth. His cry became a wail, and a warm body was placed against her breast. The ache of labor had drained her, and yet, the baby with dark curly hair like his father tugged at her heart. He lay upon her, eyes of blue staring into hers. His tiny lips parted, and she could feel the warmth of his breath against her skin. A different love bubbled through her. This was one for whom she would give her life.

A shadowy form knelt beside her. Rahab wearily turned her head, keeping her hand resting against the soft back of her son. She blinked, clearing her eyes, and smiled at Salmon. He placed a hand against her forehead, the other on the head of their son. Rahab understood the elation in his face as he stared at the infant.

"You had a rough birth." His attention turned to her.

She gave a gentle uplift to her lips. "He was eager and strong in his fight to enter our world."

"Boaz is a good name for him."

"What does it mean?"

"One of quickness and strength."

Weariness pulled her toward sleep. "A good description of our little man."

Salmon pressed a kiss against her forehead. "Sleep. I will watch over you both.

She dreamt of the river, and the delighted voice of YHWH calling her daughter.

Jewel of Jericho Kindle
http://www.amazon.com/review/create-review?&asin=B0851NFL91

Writing Jewel of Jericho started nearly five years ago. It's one I worked on and put aside, worked on then put aside again. I'm so excited with where it is now and how it's part of a larger context. *By the Fruit of Her Hands* reminds me we all have a part in God's plan. He has placed us in a position to be fruitful.

One thing you, the reader, can do is to review Jewel of Jericho. Reviews help increase awareness of our books, which helps us get even more readers. Reading your reviews helps me in my craft and encourages me to create more stories. I look forward to hearing about your favorite parts.

Jewel of Jericho is an entertaining read, but the story of Rahab has much more to offer than just entertainment. That's why I've designed a companion to the novel. *Walking the Walls of Jericho* offers book clubs and Ladies Bible studies an opportunity to ponder and discuss the significance of Rahab in the larger context of God's plan. There are discussion questions based on the book, Bible study of relevant chapters in the old and New Testaments, and some thought-provoking devotionals.

Order *Walking the Walls of Jericho* today.

Laurie Boulden is Assistant Professor of Elementary Education at Warner University. She volunteers time with youth and ladies' ministries at Trinity Baptist Church. She is a member of Word Weavers International and has attended the Florida Christian Writers Conference five years. She has won awards multiple years in the novel category for Biblical fiction, fantasy and science fiction, and contemporary romance. She won Writer of the Year in 2016. She recently completed a Master of Art in Creative Writing and English. Her interests lie in writing as well as teaching others to write. A good story deserves a good telling.

Other books by Laurie:

Hidden Gems

Made in the USA
Coppell, TX
04 June 2021